Cottage on Gooseberry Bay:

The Innocence Factor

by

Kathi Daley

This book is a work of fiction. Names, characters, places, and incidents either are products of the author's imagination or are used fictitiously. Any resemblance to actual events or locales or persons, living or dead, is entirely coincidental.

Copyright © 2025 by Katherine Daley

Version 1.0

Cottage on Gooseberry Bay

Rescue on Gooseberry Bay

Canine Courier

Klepto Kitty

Gooseberry Bay Cast

The Cottage on Gooseberry Bay Gang: Ainsley Holloway

The Peninsula Gang:

Cottage One – Avery Carmichael – FBI agent – Ainsley's sister – shares cottage with Bexley

Cottage One – Bexley (Bex) Cosgrove – co-founder of Forever Home Pet Rescue – shares cottage with Avery

Cottage Two – Parker Peterson – crime reporter for the *Seattle News*

Cottage Three – Jemma Hawthorn – computer genius – Josie's roommate – dating Cooper (Stefan and Damon – cats)

Cottage Three – Josie Wellington – owns a catering business – Jemma's roommate – dating Hudson (Stefan and Damon – cats)

Cottage Four – Ainsley Holloway – owns Ainsley Holloway Investigation – Avery's sister – dating Adam (Kai and Kallie – dogs)

Cottage Five – Cooper (Coop) Fairchild – helicopter tours – dating Jemma (Hank – dog)

Winchester Academy:

Adam Winchester – Archie's brother – academy's co-founder – dating Ainsley (Hitchcock – dog, Hercules – horse)

Archie Winchester – Adam's brother – academy's co-founder

Hudson Hanson – academy's math and computer science teacher – dating Josie

Andi Turner – academy's English and social studies teacher

Townsfolk and Others:

Remington (Remi) Beckett – owns several video game arcades – good friend to both Ainsley and Bexley

Deputy Dani Dixon – local law enforcement Gooseberry Bay

The Rescue on Gooseberry Bay Gang:

Bexley (Bex) Cosgrove

Forever Home Pet Rescue:

Bexley (Bex) Cosgrove – rescue's co-founder with best friend, Denver

Denver Marshall – rescue's co-founder with Bexley

Cassie Gibson – Denver's right-hand woman – lives with Denver at the main facility on Bainbridge Island

Ophelia Everly – works at the Seattle adoption center

Gina Jones – works at the Seattle adoption center

Poppy Hancock – runs the Gooseberry Bay adoption center

Willow Washington – second in command at the Gooseberry Bay adoption center

Lexi Hamilton – veterinarian for the main facility on Bainbridge Island

The Elderberry Bay Resort:

Unit Ten A – Gary Wild – co-owns a restaurant with Steve

Unit Ten A – Steve Donaldson – co-owns a restaurant with Gary

Unit Eleven A – Maxine (Max) Westwood – hacker with a past

Unit Eleven B – Marilyn Madison – retired actress

Unit Twelve A – Avery Carmichael

Unit Twelve A – Parker Peterson

Unit Twelve A – Bexley (Bex) Cosgrove

Unit Twelve B – Sully Rafferty – retired cop turned mystery writer

The FBI Team:

Agent Avery Carmichael

Special Agent in Charge Lake Bristow

Agent Blade Branson

Agent Dante Ryker

Townsfolk and Others:

Remington (Remi) Beckett – owns several video game arcades – good friend to both Ainsley and Bexley

Alfred Sutton – crime reporter for *Seattle News*

Deputy Dani Dixon – local law enforcement Gooseberry Bay

Ezra Reinhold – reclusive billionaire – Civilian Crime Fighter

Georgie Crawford – Remi's foster brother, disappeared in two thousand six

Chapter 1

The morning sun shone down on Gooseberry Bay, creating the illusion of tiny fireflies on the water. It was a nearly perfect day in the small town I called home. The predicted high temperatures hovered in the mid-seventies, the air was calm, and the blue sky was cloud-free as far as the eye could see.

"Morning, Ainsley," my favorite barista at the coffee cart on the boardwalk across the street from Ainsley Holloway Investigations greeted me after I stopped to order my morning latte. "Where are the kids this morning?"

I knew that by "kids," she meant my Bernese Mountain Dogs, Kai and Kallie. "I'm meeting with a new client, so I left them at Jemma and Josie's cottage." I referred to my neighbors and good friends, Jemma Hawthorn and Josie Wellington, who, along with their cats, Stefan and Damon, were happy to doggy-sit any time I needed.

"I suspect they'll have fun with the roommates. Do you want your regular?"

"I do." I knew by regular she was referring to my usual nonfat triple shot no foam latte. "It sure is a gorgeous day. I think it might be the nicest one yet this season."

She poured the milk into the machine. "It is a near-perfect day. There are cold and windy days in the early spring when I can't help but wonder why I thought an outdoor cart was a good idea, but then, on days like today, I suddenly remember why I wanted to be outside and not cooped up in a storefront all summer."

"The long-range weather forecast shows sunny and moderate days for at least the next few weeks. Of course, that could change, but I'm rooting for a long spring, followed by a mild summer."

"I hear ya." She handed me my cup. "Now that spring seems to have arrived, and the on-again/off-again rain we had last month seems to have ended, the seasonal vendors are beginning to show up. I love this time of year when the boardwalk comes to life. There are a few hearty year-round carts like me, but most choose to close down from Christmas through Memorial Day. It feels somewhat desolate in the winter, but when spring arrives, life on the boardwalk is everything I hoped it would be."

I handed the woman a twenty-dollar bill and waited for the change.

"Do you know if the shaved ice people plan to return this year?" I accepted the change and dropped a couple of bills in the tip jar.

"I heard they will be back, but I haven't seen them yet. In fact, I think most of the regular vendors will be back this year. Ivan and Glory from the little cart that sold locally sourced pottery moved into a storefront over the winter, and I heard they weren't planning to bother with a cart on the boardwalk. Doug and Levon from the hat cart decided to try their luck in Seattle, so they won't be back this season either, but I think everyone else will be returning."

"How about the brothers with the pastry cart?" I did love a sweet treat to start my day.

She frowned. "I'm not sure that I've heard one way or another. I hope they're back. Those fritters they had last season were to die for."

A line had begun to form behind me, so I decided to take my latte and walk down the boardwalk. There were a lot of vendors who had set up their carts since I'd been down to look around a week ago. I would be willing to bet that everyone with a permit to set up a cart will have done so within another week. While it was early in the day for the food carts to really ramp up, I knew that the scents of hotdogs roasting, burgers grilling, churros warming, and popcorn and nuts from the vendor near the marina, would dominate the area in a few hours, which would draw in folks passing by who didn't even realize that they were hungry until an imprinted memory from their past sent them looking for a boardwalk favorite from childhood.

"Two for twenty," a man with a purple shirt and bright green pants said as I walked by his cart featuring brightly colored visors. Given my fair skin, I owned a lot of hats and visors since keeping the sun off my face was always a good idea.

"Do you have one the color of your shirt?"

His lips turned up in a crooked grin. "I do. The visors are one for fifteen or two for twenty. Would you like to add a second color?"

"How about the bright orange one in the back."

He handed me both visors, and I gave him a twenty-dollar bill. I was about to turn around and head back to my office when I noticed Hope Masterson, the first friend I made after arriving at Gooseberry Bay and a good friend still to this day, standing in front of a cart selling freshly baked bread and bagels.

"Good morning, Hope," I said after I walked up behind her. "I see you're getting an early start on the freshly baked bread."

She turned and smiled at me. "This is one of my favorite seasonal carts, and the fresh bread, muffins, and bagels are always a hit with my guests." She looked behind me. "Kai and Kallie aren't with you?"

"Since I have a new client meeting today, I left them with Jemma and Josie. I was a few minutes early for my meeting, so I decided to walk down the boardwalk and see who had already returned." I held up my visors. "It looks like I'll have a colorful presence this year."

"They are bright, but I really like them. I feel like a splash of color is warranted after the long winter."

"I find I agree with that." I glanced at the large tote bag she carried over one shoulder. "Are you heading back to the inn or continuing onward?"

"I need to get back. I spent the morning at the high school, so I had to leave my housekeeping staff in charge of serving breakfast. I suppose I should check on things."

Hope owned the Rosewood Inn. While she didn't have school-aged children, she was active in the community and a member of multiple boards, including the school board.

"Is everything okay at the high school?" I asked. Unless something was up, it seemed somewhat early in the day for a board meeting.

"Everything's fine. Alice Cummings had her baby early. A healthy girl named Jasmine."

"I heard she was expecting. I'm glad everything went okay. Early deliveries can be tricky."

"They can be, and Jasmine was born six weeks early, so I guess the situation was dicey for a while, but I've been told the baby is fine and will be allowed to go home in a few days. I'm really happy for Alice, but taking maternity leave earlier than predicted has presented a problem with her classes. She had planned to work through the end of the term, and it hasn't been easy finding qualified substitutes this close to the end of the school year, but we finally managed to find someone who will stay through the end of the term."

Given her tone, it sounded like Hope was resigned to the situation but was less than thrilled with the substitute teacher selected. "Is there a problem with this individual?"

"Not really. It's just that I find the guy to be…" She paused as if searching for the right word, "distracting."

"Distracting?"

"He really is good-looking. I mean, 'magazine cover good-looking.' Don't get me wrong, being good-looking isn't necessarily a problem, but there's just something about this guy. I think it has something to do with his eyes that make him appear to be looking right through you. I'm not sure I can explain it, but I can't help but wonder if he was the best choice, not that we had a lot of candidates to choose from. His first day was Monday, so he's only been at the high school for a couple days, but I've been told by the principal the kids like him, and I've spoken to some of the high school staff, who have assured me that he seems to be doing his job just fine. I may not have made a connection with the guy and might not have chosen him if I'd had a choice, but we only need someone to fill in for a couple more weeks. It's not like we're trying to find the right fit for a permanent hire."

"I can understand what you're saying about a good-looking teacher being distracting. I had one of those myself when I was a student. I was a straight-A student who almost flunked history because I was too busy daydreaming about the single, twenty-six-year-old hunk at the front of the room who I was certain only had eyes for me."

She laughed. "So you do understand. If you have time, stop by the high school in the next couple of weeks and check the guy out. The guy's name is Clark Oberson, and he teaches drama, psychology, sociology, and, if I remember correctly, cultural anthropology."

"Sounds like an interesting guy. I'll look him up on the internet." I glanced at my watch. "I should get going. It was really nice chatting with you. It's been a while. Come by the peninsula and hang out sometime. We usually grill food at the roommates' cottage several times a week during the season."

"I'll give Jemma a call and arrange a time."

After I spoke to Hope, I headed directly to my office. I'd spent more time enjoying the boardwalk than I'd intended, and if I didn't want to be late for my client meeting, I would need to get a move on. My office was on Main Street, across from the boardwalk. The large picture window looking out toward the boardwalk and bay provided a lot of natural light, which was nice most days. I started brewing a pot of coffee in case my new client wanted something hot, and then I took the folder with the notes I'd taken while the woman and I chatted on the phone out of my desk drawer. What had initially sounded like a simple case had turned out to be quite interesting and unusual, to say the very least.

"Are you Ainsley Holloway?" a tall woman with wavy brown hair and bright green eyes asked after entering my office through the front door.

I stood up. "I am. And you must be Romy Mansfield. Please have a seat."

The woman was carrying a brown leather purse and a bright yellow tote bag. She set both items on the floor next to the chair and then sat down.

"Coffee?" I offered.

"No, thank you. I don't have much time since I am flying home tonight, so I'd like to get right to it."

I sat down and folded my hands on my desk. "So, how can I help you?"

She picked up the large yellow tote bag and put it on the desk. "As I briefly explained when we spoke on the phone, I found something on the bus two days ago, and I'd like you to locate the owner and return it."

"Bus?" The woman's comment surprised me because I knew that the only public bus that was available in Gooseberry Bay was the one that ran around town during the busiest summer months.

"The bus in Seattle."

I raised a brow. "Seattle?"

"I live in Virginia and have been in Seattle for the past two weeks for business. I've been taking the bus from meeting to meeting and was on my way to a meeting across town from my hotel two days ago when I entered an overly crowded bus. I didn't think there would be a place to sit, but then a lovely older woman removed the yellow tote bag she had placed next to her and put it under her seat so I could sit next to her. Since the traffic was congested and the bus was moving slowly, we started talking. I told her that I was in town on business, and she told me that while she lived in Gooseberry Bay, she was in Seattle to pick up her husband. Even though we never exchanged names, we had a lovely chat. She got off a couple stops before me, and I didn't notice that she'd left her yellow tote bag behind until I reached beneath the seat for my bag and found it there. I told the driver that the woman had left the tote bag behind, and he told me that I could set the item behind the driver's seat and that someone from the company's lost and found department would pick it up at the end of his shift. Since the woman had been so kind and placed the tote bag on the floor so I could sit down, I wanted to be sure she got it back, and my gut instinct was that the driver wasn't all that interested in making sure that happened. For some unexplained reason, I wasn't comfortable leaving the tote bag on the bus, and I decided it would be best to keep it with me and then personally hand-deliver it to the main transit office after my meeting, which I did."

The woman seemed to be taking a circuitous route to answer my question, but I knew it was important for some clients to ensure that I had the complete story, so I merely let her continue.

"When I arrived at the main transit office, I was told they would be happy to put the tote bag into lost and found. Given that it had been several hours since the woman left it behind, I figured the woman may have come in or called with an inquiry, so I asked if anyone had already come or called looking for it. They informed me they hadn't received any in-person inquiries or phone calls about a lost yellow tote bag but would hang onto it per their lost items policy."

She paused, took a breath, and then continued. "Since I'd looked inside the tote bag by this point and knew how important the contents were, I hated to leave the tote bag and its contents with the woman at the desk. I informed her that due to the importance of the contents, I'd just as soon take it with me to ensure its safety, and asked if she would take down my name and phone number so the owner could track me down if she did stop by or call, and she assured me that my plan would be fine. I was sure I'd have the tote bag returned by the end of the day, but that was two days ago, and so far, no one has come forward to claim it. As I said, since I'm due to fly out tonight, I decided that leaving the tote bag and its contents with someone I can trust to follow through and return the tote bag and its contents to its rightful owner would be the best option."

"So it occurred to you to hire a private investigator?"

She nodded. "I know that seems like an odd thing to do for a lost tote bag." She reached into the tote bag and pulled out a large pewter urn. "But I believe the woman on the bus may have left her husband behind."

Okay, I guess this was beginning to make sense.

"Are there any markings on the urn that would help us to identify its origin?"

"Not that I can tell," the woman replied. "The urn appears to be a standard container that one might use to transport ashes meant for scattering rather than saving. If I wasn't so pressed for time, I'd do additional research, but I am on an extremely tight timeline. Looking back on the conversation I had with the woman, I've decided that, while it sounded like she and her husband owned a home in Gooseberry Bay, her husband had been ill and had been either in a hospital, convalescent facility, or hospice situation in Seattle. When she said she was in town to pick him up, I guess I imagined that he had gotten better and was coming home, but after finding the urn, I realized that the woman must have actually meant that he'd died and she was in town to pick up his ashes. I can't imagine why she didn't immediately contact the transit office looking for her lost tote bag, but it's been days, and so far, if the woman who handles the desk at the main transit office is to be believed, no one has come looking for the tote bag. Given that I don't have the woman's name, address, or phone number, nor do I have time to track any of that down, this is where you come in. If you're agreeable, I want to hire you to take possession of the urn and then do your best to return the ashes to the woman who left them behind."

Since I could see that the woman was sincere in her desire to return the ashes to the woman on the bus and understood her predicament due to her imminent departure, I agreed to take possession of the urn and do my very best to return it to its rightful owner. I took down her contact information and gave her mine so we could stay in touch, and then I assured her that, given the circumstances, I would waive my regular fee. She thanked me and then left to catch the next ferry back to Seattle. Given her tight timeline, it was impressive that she'd gone to as much trouble as she had.

Once the woman left, I carefully inspected the urn. It did appear to be the sort of thing that might come standard with a cremation where the individual ordering the cremation didn't want to or have the funds to pay for a personalized urn. I imagined that the woman on the bus might be dealing with financial restraints given the fact that she likely had a mountain of medical bills to pay due to her husband's hospitalization, or as my client had indicated, she may have been planning to spread the ashes and didn't want to pay for a fancy urn that she'd have no use for in the long run.

The urn didn't appear to have any markings or identifiers I could see, so I decided the best place to start my search was at the local mortuary. But first, I had a lunch date with my boyfriend, Adam Winchester, so I locked the urn in my safe, gathered my belongings, and headed down the boardwalk toward the new café that had been opened on the pier near the marina.

Chapter 2

Since I arrived at the café about fifteen minutes early, I texted Adam to let him know I was there and planned to grab a table on the deck, and he should join me when he arrived. I ordered a freshly squeezed lemonade to sip on while I waited and then sat back to enjoy the brilliant sunshine. Tilting my head back, I closed my eyes and allowed the sun to warm my face. I'd liberally applied sunscreen that morning, and since it was a nearly perfect day, I intended to enjoy every minute of it.

"Ainsley."

I opened my eyes. "Phoenix." I stood up and hugged the young woman who'd been such a large part of my life the past few years. I'd first met Phoenix four years ago when she was still in high school. She was part of a group known as the Geek

Squad, a likable group of five friends with huge IQs and limited social skills, at least at the time. In the years I'd known her, Phoenix had grown from an awkward teen into an amazing young woman. "I didn't know you were home from college already, although now that I think about it, you did indicate that your last class would be on May the twenty-third, and here it is the twenty-eighth already. How'd your finals go?"

"They went fine. I should have straight A's again this semester, although I won't get my final grades for a few weeks. By this point, I'm just happy to be home for the summer. Last semester was intense, and I really need a mental break."

I looked around. "Are you here with friends?"

She turned and nodded toward a table where three young women were sitting. "I'm here with friends from college who are on their way to Canada for a summer program and stopped to spend the night with me on their way north. I should get back to them, but I saw you sitting here and wanted to say hi. Are you here alone?"

"I'm meeting Adam for lunch. I was a few minutes early, so I snagged a table. I don't want to keep you from your friends, but I'd love to get together soon. I want to hear about your semester and your plans for the summer."

"I'd love to get together. I actually need to talk to you about something. My friends leave tomorrow morning, although I'm not sure of the exact time they plan to leave. Maybe you and I can get together for lunch tomorrow. If my friends get a late start, it might be a late lunch, but it shouldn't be too late."

"That works for me. Once you figure out a good time to meet, text me, and we'll decide on a place to meet."

Phoenix hugged me again. "Okay, I will. I'll see you tomorrow."

She turned to return to her table just as Adam arrived. When Phoenix saw Adam, she paused to greet and hug him, and as she had with me, she expressed her desire to get together to catch up as soon as possible.

"I wasn't aware Phoenix was back already," Adam said as he kissed me on the cheek before he sat down across from me. "Skeet isn't due to arrive for another two weeks."

Skeet, who lived with Adam when he wasn't away at college, was another member of the Geek Squad.

"Her last class was this past Friday. She must have driven up right after."

"And the women she's with?"

"They're friends from college who are on their way north for a summer program."

The waitress came over, so we ordered our meal before continuing the conversation. Once the waitress had left, I asked Adam about the meeting he'd had at the high school. When I'd spoken to him that morning to lock in our plans for lunch, he mentioned that he'd had a meeting at the high school, probably the same meeting Hope had attended, but I couldn't be sure about that.

"The meeting went as well as could be expected." When Adam answered my question, a frown was on his face. "I'm not sure whether or not you heard, but Alice Cummings had her baby six weeks early, and she's unable to complete the school year as planned."

"I did hear that. I also heard that Alice's replacement is quite the looker."

Adam gave me an odd look. "I don't know about the man being quite the looker, but he does seem to be the dynamic sort with an ability to draw people in. Most people, at least. It seems that Justice has a past with the man. The context of the past is still unclear to me since neither Justice nor the new substitute teacher seemed willing to elaborate on the reason for the conflict between them. The only thing I know at this point is that Justice was up at the high school with a couple of the other kids from the academy to watch a baseball game yesterday afternoon, and the new substitute teacher, who was also at the game, said something to Justice when he walked past him. According to what others have told me, Justice went berserk, and there was a very loud verbal exchange between Justice and the new substitute teacher. I guess it got so out of hand that one of the onlookers called the police. The police broke it up, and Justice and the kids from the academy left. The meeting I attended at the high school this morning included myself, as Justice's custodial guardian, Clark Oberson, the new substitute teacher Justice argued with, the high school principal, and Dani." Adam referred to Deputy Dani Dixon, the new deputy who'd been hired after Deputy Todd had been killed the previous fall.

"Is Justice in some sort of trouble?" Justice James was a new student at Winchester Academy. He'd been a late admittance after being locked up in juvenile detention for a year. The kid was brilliant but was also a hot head with a chip on his shoulder the size of Texas. Adam didn't usually admit boys with behavior problems into the school, but he'd made an exception with Justice due to his unique circumstances. It seemed that things had gone fine so far. I couldn't imagine what sort of baggage might be between Justice and the new substitute teacher that would cause him to throw away all of the progress he'd made this past semester.

"In terms of legal action, he's not in trouble, but Dani made it crystal clear that behavior like she witnessed at yesterday's baseball game cannot happen again. She asked me to keep Justice away from the high school for the remainder of the school year, and I promised to do my best to make that happen. I knew Justice had a history of reactive behavior when I decided to admit him to the academy, but he's managed to keep his rage under control to this point. I truly hope I didn't make a mistake bringing him here."

I reached out a hand and placed it over Adam's on the table. "I don't think you made a mistake. The kid has traveled a hard road, and his behavioral issues are mostly due to the inability of the rest of the world to understand his triggers and how his past experiences have affected him. You and Archie have done wonders with that boy. Justice is a quick learner who has surpassed most of his classmates despite his late arrival, has learned to socialize with the other boys, and seems to respect the staff. Most importantly, he's come a long way in his understanding of, and control of, his own triggers since he's been with you. At this point, I can't help but wonder if we might want to assume that the outburst witnessed yesterday afternoon had as much to do with Clark Oberson as it had to do with Justice."

"Do you think that Oberson might have done something in the past that was so heinous that he actually deserved the verbal abuse Justice dealt him?"

I shrugged. "Perhaps. I ran into Hope, who shared that she found the man distracting. She made an offhanded comment about his looks being the distracting factor, but I picked up on this vibe when she mentioned the guy. If I had to guess, I would say something about him disturbed her. And not just his looks. Hope is the intuitive sort who has an excellent 'feel' for people. I think her comment came more from that than anything."

"The guy did have an odd sort of stare, and his eyes…" Adam let the sentence dangle while he appeared to gather his thoughts. "There was something off about his eyes. It's not that anything is physically wrong with his eyes; it's just that he has this intensity that I can't quite explain."

"Hope said much the same thing about his eyes."

"I can understand how the guy might have set Justice off, but that doesn't mean Justice's behavior can be tolerated."

"I agree. Is there a plan to deal with the fallout from Justice's outburst?"

Adam blew out a long breath before he answered. "Archie asked that I allow him to speak to Justice, and I agreed to do things his way. Archie can be a bit too lenient with the boys, but he cares about them, and they seem to care about him in return, which keeps them from running all over my soft-hearted brother. While I'd normally say that a behavioral outburst such as that witnessed yesterday would require a sizable penalty rather than a softly delivered speech by Archie about understanding motives and dealing with consequences, in this case, Justice has had to deal with more than his fair share of hammers in his life, so maybe a soft approach will work best."

Justice's mother died when he was young. He grew up with an alcoholic father and an older sister who tried to fill the void left by their mother's death to the best of her ability. Two years ago Justice's sister, Lydia, a high school junior, was strangled and left for dead beneath the bleachers of the high school she attended in Tacoma. Her boyfriend, Roger, was the prime suspect, but he seemed to have an alibi, so while he was questioned, he was never arrested. The case grew cold, and an arrest was never made. Justice had been in the eighth grade at the time. His father remained his legal guardian, but he was rarely around to do any parenting. When Justice entered high school, he fell in with a rowdy crowd. He was arrested a few times for minor infractions, such as underage drinking, shoplifting, and possession of a controlled substance by a minor. He ended up in the juvenile detention center for a year, which is when Adam received a letter from Justice's parole officer asking him to consider Justice for his program. Adam contacted one of his teachers, who indicated that Justice had a brilliant mind, which was on the verge of being lost in the system, and that what he really needed was someone to take him under their wing and help mold him into the man the teacher knew he could be. Adam agreed to meet the boy, and after they had engaged in a long conversation, committed to accepting Justice into the academy once the boy had completed his sentence. He'd been with Adam since February, and things had gone even better than expected, at least so far.

The conversation was interrupted when the waitress came by with our meal. When the conversation resumed, the topic segued onto the topic of my new client. I explained the situation to Adam and then asked for his input.

"If the urn isn't marked, it won't be easy to find the woman who left it on the bus, but not impossible," he said. "We know that the woman had the urn on the bus two days ago, and if she lived in Gooseberry Bay and only went to Seattle to collect the ashes, that would likely mean that her husband has passed away within the last week or so. While I realize it's not an address, it is a place to start."

"How many crematoriums do you think there are in Seattle?" I asked.

"No idea, but we can narrow things down. We can assume that the woman walked onto the ferry to come across since your client met her on the bus, which would indicate she didn't have a car. Since she had the urn with her, which appears to indicate that she had recently picked it up, it can be assumed that she had used a service in the downtown area. I imagine that there will only be one, maybe two, mortuaries that meet that criteria."

"That's a good point. Rather than calling all the mortuaries in the area, I can start by calling the one closest to where my client met the woman." I smiled. "Thanks. For some reason, I was complicating things in my mind. I'd even planned to visit our local mortuary after lunch, but she wouldn't have used the local guy if she was in Seattle with the ashes."

"I'm happy that I could help." He popped a piece of crab into his mouth. "This seafood salad is outstanding. The seafood tastes like it was caught yesterday rather than left in a freezer for months and months."

"I don't know about it being caught yesterday, but I agree that it's very fresh and delicious. And the dressing is really unique."

Adam held up the breadbasket. "Another roll?"

"No. I think I'll save room for the cookout tonight. Are you planning to attend?"

Our friends, Jemma and Josie, had texted the entire group earlier to let everyone know they'd be grilling steaks if anyone wanted to come by.

"I think I will plan to come by for dinner. Given the situation with Justice, I may not stay over tonight. I know Archie wanted to be the one to talk to him, and I know I agreed to his request, but I am the one who went to the meeting at the high school, so I would like to fill Archie in on the discussion that was had sooner rather than later."

"I'm sorry you can't stay, but I understand."

"Assuming, of course, that Justice understands what he needs to do and will agree to stay at the academy and avoid town until things calm down, maybe I can plan to spend the weekend on the peninsula."

I smiled. "Spending the weekend together would be nice. I'll pencil you in."

While the phrase "I'll pencil you in" was a bit of a joke between Adam and me, the reality was that between his commitment to the Winchester Foundation and the Winchester Academy and my job as a private investigator, our plans usually were soft. Given that it wasn't uncommon for one or both of us to need to cancel at the last minute, we both knew that was always a possibility, and we tried not to let things like scheduling define our relationship or the importance of our commitment to each other.

Chapter 3

After sharing lunch with Adam, I decided it would be a good time to begin working on my new client's case, so I returned to my office. Adam had made a good point when he said that the mortuary used by the woman on the bus to have her husband cremated was most likely close to the area where my client had encountered the woman. I logged into my computer and Googled crematoriums in the area and found only one. That seemed like as good a place as any other to start my search, so I called the number on the ad and waited for someone to answer the phone.

"Hi," I said to the woman who answered after she rattled off the name of the mortuary. "My name is Ainsley Holloway. I'm a private investigator based in Gooseberry Bay. I've been hired by a temporary visitor to the Seattle area to track down a woman she met on a bus. It seems the woman my client has been trying to track down left her tote bag on the bus two days ago, and an urn with what we believe to be her husband's ashes is inside the tote bag. I hoped you could help me track down the woman who left the tote bag behind."

"Have you contacted the transit office? They have a lost and found."

"My client did speak to the staff at the main transit office, but so far, no one has come forward looking for the tote bag with the urn inside, which I will admit is odd. It seems to me that if I left the ashes of my dead husband on a bus, calling to check lost and found would be the first thing I would do. At this point, I can only assume that something has happened to prevent the woman on the bus from looking for her misplaced tote bag." I hoped the woman had merely forgotten where she left her tote bag and had not met with any foul play. "Anyway, the urn I have is pewter and free of markings. Since the woman on the bus chose not to pay for engraving, there isn't a way for me to determine with any degree of certainty where the urn came from or whose ashes it contained. Your place of operation is the closest to the bus line where my client ran into the elderly woman riding on the bus, so I decided to start here."

"I'll need you to describe the woman with the urn and the exact date she was seen on the bus with it."

Based on the information provided by my client during our initial interview, I did as the woman on the phone requested. This seemed to be enough information for the woman on the phone to confirm that the body of a deceased had been processed by their staff and released to the wife of the deceased less than an hour before my client ran into the woman who'd traveled from Gooseberry Bay to Seattle to pick up her husband's remains. I asked the woman on the phone for the name and contact information of the woman who'd picked up the ashes, and this was when she'd waffled.

"I'm not sure I should release that information to a stranger on the phone. While it sounds as if your reason for wanting to contact this woman is honorable, the reality is that you're just a voice on the phone. Honestly, for all I know, you could be anyone, and your actual reason for wanting to track down this woman could be less honorable than you've indicated."

"I understand," I said. "What do you need from me? Do you want me to send you a copy of my PI license? Or would you prefer to video chat so you can get a look at me?"

"I'd prefer the request for information come from the police. If you really are a private investigator, you must have contacts in law enforcement."

"I do. My sister is an agent for the Seattle office of the FBI, but she's out of town on a case. If I have one of the agents in her office call you, will you provide the information I need?"

"If they'll email me a copy of their ID, I'll call you back with the information you need."

It took a while, but I finally tracked down Agent Dante Ryker, a friend and a member of Avery's FBI team who had helped us in the past. I explained the situation, and he assured me he would contact the mortuary and request the information I needed to locate the woman my client met on the bus. Once I had the name and address of the woman from the bus, I locked up my office and headed toward her residence. I'd hoped she'd be home and that I could arrange to return her property to her, but when I arrived at the white house with the blue trim and slightly overgrown garden, I found it locked up tight.

"Excuse me," I said to the neighbor next door who was watering her potted plants. "I'm looking for Deborah Goldfield and hoped you could help me."

"You have the right house, but Deborah took the ferry to Seattle to pick up her husband's ashes two days ago. I thought she would return that same day, but I haven't seen her since."

"I see. I don't suppose you have Deborah's cell phone number. I have something of hers that was left on the bus, and I'd really like to return it."

The woman turned the water to her hose off. "I have her number inside. Hang on, and I'll get it."

I thanked the woman and then called Deborah. When the call went straight to voicemail, I left a message. The urn was tucked safely inside the safe in my office, so I figured that there was no real urgency here today. If Deborah hadn't returned my call by tomorrow, I would put more effort into tracking her down. In the meantime, I had a cookout at the roommates' cottage to get to this evening.

There were five cottages on the peninsula where I lived. My sister, Avery, shared Cottage One with our good friend and animal rescue worker, Bexley Cosgrove. Neither was currently present in Gooseberry Bay, but the cottage was occupied by one or the other most of the time.

My good friend and newspaper reporter, Parker Peterson, occupied Cottage Two. She hadn't been around for more than a week, but the last time I spoke to her, she had mentioned her intent to spend time on our side of the Sound this week.

Cottage Three was occupied by two roommates, Jemma Hawthorne and Josie Wellington. and their cats, Stefan and Damon. Jemma was a software developer who worked from home, and Josie owned a mobile catering business.

I lived in Cottage Four with my dogs, Kai and Kallie, and Jemma's boyfriend, Cooper Fairchild, lived in Cottage Five with his dog, Hank.

Those who resided on the peninsula were as much a family as any blood-related family. Adam was considered an honorary family member since he and I were involved in a committed relationship. Josie's boyfriend, Hudson Hanson, who taught math and computer science at Winchester Academy, had recently achieved family status, too.

"I'm back," I called out after letting myself into the roommates' cottage. Kai and Kallie came running to greet me, just as Jemma had called out to let me know they were outside on the deck. While all the cottages on the peninsula had decks with views of

Gooseberry Bay, the roommates' cottage and mine were the only ones on the shoreline, providing the best water views you would likely get anywhere in the area.

"So, how'd it go?" Jemma asked after I sat on a chair between Jemma and Josie. I knew she was wondering about the meeting with my new client, so I filled the roommates in.

"Wow. That is so odd," Josie said. "I can't imagine why this woman wouldn't be doing more to find her husband's ashes unless something happened to her after she got off of the bus."

"I agree and am beginning to think that something has happened to Deborah. Not only has she not bothered to contact the main transit office about the tote bag she left on the bus, but I spoke to her neighbor, who confirmed that Deborah headed toward Seattle on the ferry two days ago intending to pick up her husband's ashes and planning to return to Gooseberry Bay later that same day. She hasn't seen her since. I'm wondering whether or not I should file a missing persons report, but honestly, I don't have enough information about the woman to even provide a dependable description."

"Maybe the neighbor can help with that," Josie suggested.

"Maybe," I agreed.

Jemma offered me a glass of iced tea, which I accepted.

"Maybe Avery can help." Jemma referred to my sister.

"As far as I know, Avery is still in Alaska," I responded.

"She's been gone a long time. At least a month," Jemma replied.

"She has been, and so far, she hasn't indicated when she might be back," I said. "Since I know behavior like this isn't out of character for her, I'm trying not to worry, but I must admit that I'll feel better when she gets home." I paused to think about things. "I suppose I might try calling Ryker and see if he can help me track down this woman. He's helped us with cases in the past."

"I heard he and Parker are dating," Josie said.

"As far as I know, they aren't dating, but they are friends," I corrected. "Contentious friends."

Jemma laughed. "Knowing Parker, contentious friends sounds like the recipe for a romance in the making to me."

Knowing Parker and her taste in men who challenged her, Jemma likely wasn't that far off.

"Deborah's neighbor gave me her cell phone number," I informed the others. "I called and left a message, letting her know I had her tote bag and its contents, and asked her to call me. If she doesn't call me back by tomorrow, I'll put more effort into tracking her down. I could call Agent Ryker, who was actually the one who got me her contact information in the first place, or I could call Parker and ask for her help. She has lots of connections in the city that I don't have. Perhaps she can convince the local PD to keep an eye out for her."

"That might be a good idea," Jemma agreed. "If the woman is in trouble, we might be the only people who even realize she's missing."

Jemma made a good point.

"Maybe you should call the hospitals in the area now that you have a name," Josie suggested. "It seems to me that the woman from the bus would be actively looking for her husband's ashes if she was physically able to."

"That's a good idea," I said. "In fact, I'm going to go ahead and make a couple calls now."

I contacted every hospital and clinic within a twenty-mile radius of where Deborah was last seen by my client. No one claimed to have admitted anyone with that name. The individuals I spoke with, like my friends, suggested that I call the police if I didn't track down my friend, but since I still wasn't sure about doing that, I decided to call Parker. She didn't answer, so I left a message. Fifteen minutes later, she called back, letting me know she was off today and hanging out with Ryker. She promised to dive deeper and see what she could discover about Deborah Goldfield's current whereabouts.

Once I completed my calls, I returned to the roommates' deck to find that Coop and Hank had arrived. I greeted both the man and his nearly blind dog. Due to his disability, Hank's world had been exceedingly small when Bexley first placed Hank with Coop, but Hank appeared to be thriving after spending five months with Coop.

"Is Adam going to show?" Coop asked after he kissed Jemma hello and took a seat.

"He'll be by shortly," I assured him.

"And Hudson is on his way," Josie joined in.

Coop was the only male living on the peninsula, so I imagined he appreciated it when Adam and Hudson were around.

"By the way," I said. "I ran into Hope today and told her about our cookouts and suggested she come by since it's been forever since she hung out with us. While Hope indicated that she might do that, she didn't make a firm commitment."

"She should totally come by," Josie said. "I'm going to call her and see if I can seal the deal."

"It would be nice to catch up with Hope," Jemma said after Josie excused herself to make the call. "She used to hang out here with us all the time, but now I only see her when there's some sort of volunteer thing she needs help with."

"She does seem to be a lot busier than she used to be," I agreed.

"I think she stopped coming around when Tegan and Booker began to have problems," Coop said. "Tegan was her best friend, but she was also close to Booker, and I don't think she wanted to get pulled into the middle of things."

I found that I couldn't blame her for feeling that way. The Tegan Walker, Booker Maguire, Jackson Davidson love triangle had been a gigantic mess, and while I did miss my friends, I was as happy as anyone that the drama had ended when both Tegan and Booker moved away.

When Josie returned to the group, she announced that Hope planned to stop by and, in fact, was on her way over now. She planned to stay for dinner so she'd have a chance to really catch up with us. Of course, as we should have anticipated, Josie indicated that Hope had a fabulous volunteer opportunity to discuss with us, which could always be expected when the town's busy summer season was just around the corner. I wasn't sure how the whole thing came about, but somehow, Hope had taken on the task of volunteer coordinator for the entire town. In a small town where every day was an opportunity to celebrate, organizing the volunteers wasn't an easy job.

"Do we know which upcoming event she's recruiting help for?" I asked, wanting to be mentally prepared with my availability.

"She mentioned that she needed help for the annual Movies on the Beach event the town holds every other Friday during the summer, as well as the Fourth of July event."

The Movies on the Beach event featured a different movie, which was shown on a massive screen made out of an old sail down on Land's End Beach every other Friday from the last Friday in June through the last Friday in August. Movies on the

Beach was a free event, and the movies were definitely not new releases, but it was fun to watch films from the eighties and nineties under the stars. It was also somewhat romantic since the movie didn't start until after it was completely dark. The Fourth of July event tended to be a community-wide draw with a pancake breakfast, followed by a parade down Main Street, bands, and a kiddie carnival in the park. Of course, the main attraction was the fireworks show over the bay, which always proved to be an event worth staying up for.

"I'm in for both," I said. "The Movies on the Beach event is always a lot of fun, and I know how important the funds raised at the Fourth of July event are for the town."

"I'm in as well," Jemma said. "I'm somewhat surprised Hope isn't recruiting volunteers for the Halloween event. It's never too early to start lining folks up for the haunted house."

"I'm sure she won't hesitate to bring that up, too," Josie assured us.

As expected, after she arrived, the first thing Hope did was pass around a sign-up sheet for volunteer duties for all three events we'd talked about. Once that was done, she hinted that the one thing she needed the most was a coordinator for the Halloween event, but no one volunteered, so she moved on. Hope was still in the process of catching us up about some of the changes to our local events suggested at the last community event meeting when Parker returned my call. I got up and went inside to take it.

"Hey. Did you find Deborah?" I asked.

"Maybe. Probably. What Ryker and I found was a Jane Doe who was admitted to the hospital less than two hours after your client last saw Deborah. She appears to have been the victim of a mugging and was unconscious upon arrival at the hospital. She wasn't carrying an ID, and her prints didn't match any in the database. They took a DNA sample but haven't received any matches yet."

"She doesn't know who she is?" I asked.

"She still hasn't regained consciousness, although the doctor Ryker spoke to did say that she's been drifting in and out of consciousness all day today. I know you never actually saw this woman, but your client did. Do you think that she'd be willing to ID her from a photo?"

"I think she would. Text a photo to me, and I'll text it to her."

"Just be warned. The poor thing is pretty beat up. Deborah has abrasions on her face, but I think your client will still be able to discern her features well enough to ID her."

Parker forwarded the photo to me, and then I called my client, explained the situation, and forwarded the photo to her. She verified that the Jane Doe in the hospital was the woman on the bus, who we now knew was Deborah Goldfield. I called Parker back, and she promised to keep in touch regarding Deborah's condition. I assured Parker I had the ashes and would keep them safe until Deborah could collect them.

Adam and Hudson had arrived by the time I returned to the deck. The men were filling the group in on the situation with Justice. Even though I'd already heard most of what was being discussed from Adam at lunch, it was interesting to hear everyone's individual take on things.

"Justice isn't a bad kid," Hudson said as I settled on a chair. "He's just had a hard life. The sort of hard life that might make anyone lash out occasionally."

"I heard that his mother died when he was just a kid," Jemma said.

Hudson confirmed that to be true. "Then, in addition to that," Hudson added, "Justice's sister was murdered two years ago. She was strangled and left for dead beneath the bleachers at the high school she attended. Justice was just thirteen at the time. His sister had been both a sister and mother to him. Her murder hit him hard."

Everyone agreed that something like that would affect even the most stable individual.

Hudson moved on and began to discuss Justice's juvey record and his time in lock up. He'd described the chip the kid had on his shoulder when he first arrived at Winchester Academy, but Hudson assured everyone that Justice had found his way since he'd been there and that, in many ways, the boy was a totally different kid. Hudson admitted that he didn't fully understand what had made Justice lash out to the degree he had. Hudson also assured everyone that after Archie had chatted with Justice, the boy admitted he realized that he had likely blown all the progress he had made since he'd been here in Gooseberry Bay. Justice promised to avoid the high school and the new substitute teacher.

"It sounds to me that this new substitute teacher has a secret that not everyone knows about," Josie said. "Justice can be reactive at times, and he undeniably struggles with anger issues, but I agree with Hudson when he says that Justice is a good kid. If asked for my opinion, I'd say that the fact that he went off on the new substitute teacher the way he did says that Justice knows something the rest of us don't."

"If Justice knows something the rest of us don't, why wouldn't he fill us in?" Hope asked.

Josie admitted that she didn't know, but she was the loyal sort. If she'd decided to have Justice's back, you could count on her to have it no matter what might occur from this point forward.

Chapter 4

The cookout the previous evening had been a lot of fun, but, unfortunately, I'd stayed up much later than I'd planned, which made getting up early to run with the dogs before I headed into town much more challenging than usual. When the alarm went off, I was tempted to go back to sleep and save my run for another day, but the thought of a spring sunrise on what had promised to be a perfectly sunny day was more than I could resist, so I rolled out of bed and got into my running gear.

The sky had just begun to lighten when we exited the cottage through the front door. My jog started slowly as the dogs and I ran along the southernmost tip of the bay. When we reached Main Street, we crossed over and continued up the hill toward the high school. I knew the sun would come up over the bluff to the east of us, and if I timed it right, I could watch the sun rising from a vantage point above the bay. Generally speaking, seeing a sunrise from this vantage point provided a brilliant display as the colorful sky reflected artfully on the perfectly calm water.

Once we reached the high school's parking lot, we continued to jog around the buildings. The football and baseball fields and the running track, where I enjoyed running sprints, could be found on the hill at the rear of the buildings. The fields sat up high enough that a view of the bay over the top of the school's infrastructure was possible. Once I reached the running track, which was the furthest up the hillside, I paused to enjoy the first rays of sunshine as the ball of orange poked its head above the horizon.

"It's going to be another near-perfect day," I said to the dogs as we watched the ball of orange climb into the sky. "It's days like this that make me grateful to live in such a gorgeous location."

Kallie put a paw on my knee. She knew I was speaking to her, but since she likely had no idea what I was saying, the paw to the knee was her way of letting me know she was listening even though, as far as she was concerned, the words I was speaking were nothing more than gibberish.

After watching the gorgeous sunrise, I chose to run a few laps around the track before heading back toward the cottage. Being large dogs, Kai and Kallie weren't equipped to run all out, even for short distances, which made the track the perfect place for me to run circles around them while they hung out on the grass in the center of the field. As I rounded the southernmost end of the track for the second time, I noticed that the dogs had left their resting place in the center of the field. I stopped running.

"Kai. Kallie," I called.

Kallie came jogging back from beneath the bleachers. Kai didn't follow. I headed in that direction.

"What's going on?" I asked Kallie. The dogs were well-trained and didn't just wander off often.

Kallie headed back under the bleachers, and I followed. It was then that I noticed Kai and the very dead body he was standing watch over.

After checking for a pulse, just in case, I pulled my cell phone out of my pocket and called nine-one-one. I was told to wait where I was for the emergency personnel to arrive. I agreed to do so, and then I called Adam.

"It's Clark Oberson," I said as I attempted to comprehend what I'd observed. "He's dead."

"Dead?" Adam said in a voice a bit louder than his usual tone. "Dead, how?"

I glanced back toward the body. "I'm not sure. The dogs and I came to the high school to do some laps and watch the sunrise, and we found the new substitute teacher beneath the bleachers. I haven't touched the body other than to check for a pulse. I didn't notice any blood, but his death didn't seem natural either. Maybe drugs or maybe strangulation." I paused and took a deep breath. "I'm really not sure.

The police are on the way. I was told to wait, which is what I'm doing."

"Is there anyone else in the area?" Adam asked.

"Not that I saw. The dogs would have alerted me if there had been someone else nearby, so I'm going to say that if there had been someone with Mr. Oberson when he died, they're gone now."

"I'm on my way. I'll ride Hercules, which will be quicker than taking the long way around in the car."

I could hear the tension in his voice.

"You really don't need to come. I'm fine."

"I should be there. At this point, I haven't jumped to any conclusions, but Justice didn't come home last night."

This was the point when I was sure my heart skipped a beat. "Justice isn't with you at the academy?"

"When I got home from the cookout last night, Archie told me that Justice and one of the other boys had argued and that the argument had turned physical, and punches were exchanged. He sent both boys to their rooms. This isn't the first time Justice has been given a time-out due to inappropriate behavior, so I wasn't worried about it and just went to bed. But when he didn't show up for breakfast this morning, I went to his room to check on him. He wasn't there, and the bed hadn't been slept in."

"You don't think…"

50

"I hope not. I'm leaving now. I should be there in twenty minutes."

After I hung up, I looked toward the road leading up the hill from town. I could hear sirens in the distance, which seemed unnecessary at this point since the man was already dead, and there wasn't a lot of urgency. Still, I supposed that a dead body under the bleachers at the high school was a big deal for a small town like Gooseberry Bay, and it did make sense that law enforcement would want to arrive before the students began to show up for their classes. Deputy Dani Dixon, the first law enforcement officer to arrive at the high school, made her way over to where I was waiting. Three other vehicles pulled in behind her.

"Are you the one who found the deceased?" she asked after she'd paused just a few seconds to say hi to the dogs.

"I am. The body is under the bleachers. It's the new substitute teacher, Clark Oberson."

"Did you notice anyone else in the area when you arrived?"

"No. It was quiet when the dogs and I got here before sunrise."

"Okay. Wait right here. I'll check it out and then be back to talk to you."

I nodded as Deputy Dixon walked away. When the female deputy had first been hired to replace a long-time Gooseberry Bay resident, Deputy Todd, after he'd been murdered, I hadn't been sure about her. But I'd gotten to know her since she'd been in town, and from what I could tell, unlike her predecessor, she was an honest cop who truly cared about the people she served. My good friend, Remington Beckett, Remi to most, had actually developed a friendship with the woman, and Remi had assured me that Dani seemed open-minded and could be trusted.

Adam arrived riding his horse, Hercules, before Deputy Dixon had returned to speak to me. The dogs and I had found a nice patch of grass to wait on where we were out of the way but were still able to see what was happening. Adam tied Hercules to a tree and then wandered over to wrap me in a hug.

"Any word about the cause of death?" he asked.

"No. I don't know anything more than I did when we spoke on the phone. Deputy Dixon and three other deputies went to look at the body. I was instructed to wait, but no one has come to speak to me yet. I did notice one of the deputies with Dixon call for the coroner. Once he gets here to take possession of the body, I imagine someone will be over to interview me."

Adam looked toward the bleachers but didn't respond.

"Are you going to tell them that Justice snuck out last night and still hasn't come home?" I asked.

He frowned. "I don't know. I thought about that very question on my ride over. If I am specifically asked about Justice, I will tell the truth, but I'm not sure how I feel about bringing it up if the question isn't asked."

"If he's innocent, it won't matter if Deputy Dixon knows he was missing. In fact," I added, "at this point, we don't even know for sure if he's okay."

Adam bobbed his head slightly. "Yeah. That's a good point. At this time, I guess telling Dixon what is going on with Justice is the best move. If Justice is innocent, he'll have an explanation as to where he's been once he shows up, and if the boy is guilty, then I guess he'll need to face the consequences of his actions."

"Do you think there is any possibility that he's guilty?"

Adam hesitated before answering. "I'd like to say I was as confident as Archie that the boy could never do anything like this, but I'd be lying if I said that it hasn't crossed my mind that he might have."

I looked around. "Where is Archie? I thought he might come with you."

"He's looking for Justice. Hudson and Andi are interviewing all the boys, and Archie is physically tracking down every lead." Andi Turner taught literature, history, and the social arts at Winchester Academy. "Whether Justice is innocent or guilty, Archie and I think it will be best for us to find him before the authorities do."

I supposed I had to agree with that. Whatever the truth, it seemed imperative that Justice had people who cared about him present when he was officially interviewed, which I was sure he would be.

About thirty minutes after Adam arrived, Deputy Dixon came to speak to us. I didn't have much to add to my statement about coming to the high school for an early morning jog and finding the body. As he said he would, Adam filled the deputy in on the fact that, while he was in no way indicating that he believed Justice was guilty of killing the man, assuming, of course, that the man had been murdered and hadn't died of natural causes, Justice was missing, and, therefore, Adam would be unable to bring him in for an interview until he was found. I could tell by the look on the deputy's face that, even if Justice was innocent, leaving the academy and not returning hadn't helped his case at all.

By the time Deputy Dixon released us to go, it was after ten o'clock. Adam needed to return to the academy since he had Hercules with him, and I had a lunch date with Phoenix, which I would hate to miss, so we agreed to stay in touch and maybe even get together later that afternoon. Whether Justice was found or not, my gut instinct told me we were in for a bumpy ride.

Chapter 5

Phoenix and I decided to grab deli sandwiches and eat them in the park overlooking the bay. It was such a pleasant day that eating indoors seemed like a sin, and the deli across from the boardwalk had freshly baked bread and quality meat and cheese, making it a good option for any day.

"So what's up?" I asked Phoenix, getting right to the point. I could have asked her about school or her plans for the summer or any one of a dozen things, but she seemed nervous and angsty when she arrived for our meet-up, so I decided to get whatever was on her mind out of the way.

"It's Riley."

Riley was Phoenix's younger sister. She'd just turned eighteen and would graduate high school in two weeks.

"What's going on with Riley?" I asked. As most sisters do, Phoenix and Riley occasionally argued, but generally, they appeared to get along well.

She paused, biting her lip in such a manner as to suggest that she might be thinking things over. Finally, she spoke. "It's not Riley so much as Ralston."

"Ralston? The name doesn't sound familiar."

"Ralston is my mother's new boyfriend."

I'd heard that Phoenix's parents' divorce had been finalized over the winter. Based on what I'd heard, the divorce had been amicable, but I supposed something like that would still be hard on the children. "Riley and Ralston don't get along?"

"It's not that they don't get along; it's that they get along too well."

I just waited.

Phoenix continued. "My mother began dating this Ralston guy a few months ago, and from the minute he came into the picture, he seems to be the only thing Riley can talk about. At first, I was glad Riley got along so well with our mother's new guy. It would have been hard on the entire family if there had been conflict. Then I came home over spring break and finally met the guy. Not only is he younger than my mother, but he really is good-looking. It's not that being good-looking in and of itself is a problem, but when I was home for spring break, I noticed that Riley seemed to have a little crush on the guy. He treated her as one should treat the daughter of one's girlfriend, and there didn't seem to be anything inappropriate going on, so I decided Riley's crush would play itself out, and there would be nothing to worry about. Then, I came home for the summer a few days ago and noticed that Riley's infatuation appeared to have deepened. Again, I want to say right up front that I haven't noticed even one thing that would point toward impropriety on Ralston's part, but I can't shake this feeling that something more is going on there. I decided to look into the guy. Do a background check."

"And?" I asked. Phoenix was a genius who knew her way around a computer, and there was no question in my mind that she could easily handle running a rather extensive background check.

"And I think I was right to be concerned."

I frowned. "And what did you find?"

It looked like she was preparing to respond, but then she closed her mouth. She appeared to be either confused or conflicted, perhaps both.

"Did you find something that has led to this meeting?" I tried again.

"I'm not sure. I realize this sounds somewhat odd, but it's not so much what I found as it is what I haven't been able to find."

"Okay," I said. "What haven't you found?"

"A personal history, for one thing. The guy told my mother that his name was Ralston Richardson. He told her that he moved to Gooseberry Bay from a small rural town in Utah to take a job as a geologist in the area. I asked him a few general questions about geology in our area, and he quickly changed the subject. My gut instinct tells me that the guy knows less about geology than I do, and trust me, I don't know a lot. But the thing is, if Ralston is lying about why he's in the area, why would he choose such a specific career if he knew nothing about it? Why not just say he was a dock worker or a tree trimmer? That part makes no sense."

I had to agree with that.

"And then there is the fact that nothing came up when I looked up Ralston Richardson of Panguitch, Utah. He had mentioned that he moved around a lot and hadn't lived there long, so I went broader and searched the Utah DMV for someone with that name. I got four hits. All four were men in their fifties through their seventies. Ralston never told me his age, but I'd guess he falls somewhere in the thirty to thirty-five age range."

"If the guy moves around a lot, maybe he simply never got around to changing his driver's license from the state he previously lived to the state he moved into."

"Maybe," she said, although she looked doubtful. "I asked Ralston if he'd always been a geologist, and he said he was a long-haul trucker before he decided to complete his degree in geology. I asked who he worked for, and he said something about having his own rig. I then pretended to be fascinated by the idea of taking to the road and doing the long-haul thing, and he shared a few quips, which led me to believe he might actually have been a trucker at one point. A geologist, however? I really don't think so."

I took a sip of my iced tea before I responded. "So what I'm hearing you say is that you are concerned about Riley and the crush she seems to have on your mother's new boyfriend. Not only is this guy your mother's boyfriend, but he's much older than Riley, and he seems to have a cloudy past. You've done some preliminary research, and the results are inconclusive. While you haven't found any obvious red flags, such as a police record, you haven't found documentation that would normally be part of someone's history."

"Exactly. I know I might be way off base here. On the surface, Ralston seems like a good guy, and my mom adores him. I suppose Riley isn't the first young woman to develop a crush on her mother's good-looking boyfriend, but I just have this feeling that something isn't right. I'm pretty good at digging up what I'm looking for out of the computer, but I'm not the best at developing a strategy. I was hoping that you would help me with that. Between us, we should be able to find out who this guy is and what sort of past he's actually had."

"I'd be happy to help you," I assured Phoenix. "I do have a bit of a situation today I may need to deal with," I explained about Justice and his link to the dead substitute teacher at the high school.

"Wow. I'm so sorry. I hadn't heard. You could have just canceled this lunch."

"There was no way I was going to cancel this lunch. You are a very important person to me. Your instincts are exceptional, and if your gut instinct tells you this guy is trouble, I would believe it."

She smiled. "Thanks, Ainsley."

"I have a few things to follow up on today, but why don't you come by my cottage in the morning. Say around nine. I'll text you to confirm after I see how today goes, but at this point, tomorrow should work for me. We'll dig around and see what we can find. In the meantime, I'll ask Jemma to do some digging. You know how good she is at pulling a rabbit from a hat."

"She is one of the best."

"Do you know the make and model of Ralston's vehicle?"

"Black Ford truck. I think it's an F-250. I don't know what year."

"Do you know the license plate number?"

"No, but I'll find out and send it to you in a text."

"How about a local address?"

"I don't remember if he's ever mentioned where he lives."

"I can probably find out. Text me if you think of anything else, and we'll connect by text later. Maybe after dinner."

"That sounds good. And thanks again."

I decided to return to my cottage after my lunch with Phoenix. Jemma had the dogs again, and I figured I should relieve her. Additionally, I wanted to catch her up on my lunch with Phoenix and ask if she had any news about the situation with Justice. I suspected that Hudson and Josie had been in constant contact all morning, so the odds were that Jemma and Josie would have an update.

"So, how was lunch?" Jemma asked when I returned to the peninsula.

"It was nice. Phoenix needs our help with a project, which I will tell you about once I get an update on Justice."

"I just spoke to Josie, who is at the academy with Hudson. Thankfully, they found Justice, and he's fine. Archie found him hanging out in Remi's video arcade. Remi isn't in town this week, but I guess Remi and Justice have become more like friends than mere acquaintances, and Justice likes to hang out there. Anyway, Justice swore he had no idea that Clark Oberson was dead and that the only reason he'd taken off and come into town via the bluff trail last night was because he was upset about his argument with his fellow student and needed to clear his head."

I put my purse on the sofa close to Damon, who'd found a sunny place to sleep. "I suppose that makes sense, but where was he all night?"

"He told Archie he slept in the park. It was a decently warm night last night, and the kid has lived on the street before, so I suppose the explanation of his whereabouts is plausible."

I supposed it was plausible, but sleeping in the park wouldn't provide an alibi for Justice. "Has he spoken to Dani?" I was almost afraid to hear that he was in jail.

"He has. According to Josie, who spoke to Hudson, who spoke to Adam, Dani questioned Justice, who swore he only left the academy to have space to think things over and had nothing to do with Oberson's death. Dani didn't arrest Justice, but she did read him the riot act. She made him swear he would stay at the academy until this all gets sorted out, and then she released him into Adam's care."

"The fact that Justice took off last night and was on his own without an alibi will definitely be a tough obstacle to overcome if Dani decides to arrest him at some point."

Jemma agreed with that. She also suggested I call Adam if I wanted a first-person update, which I assured her I would. But first, she wanted to hear about Phoenix and the problem she needed help with.

Jemma frowned after I filled her in. "Phoenix has good instincts. On the surface, it sounds as if things are legitimate; however, like her, I'm not entirely convinced. I'll do some digging and see what I can find. You said Phoenix is coming by tomorrow morning."

I nodded. "I thought we could chat before the day got too crazy. I'm supposed to call her later today to check in, and if you have questions for her, I'm sure she'd be happy to tell you what she knows."

"Okay. I'll work on this for a few hours or until Josie comes home. Once Josie returns, I'm sure she'll present a plan to find Oberson's real killer as a means of helping Justice get out of a sticky situation, and she will want my help."

"Finding the real killer isn't a bad plan," I agreed. "Assuming Justice is innocent but appears to be guilty, and Dani doesn't find the real killer right away, thereby removing Justice from the suspect list."

"At this point, I suppose waiting for an update once Josie gets home rather than trying to figure things out now would be our best course of action. In the meantime, I'll start digging into Clark Oberson. If we can get to know the victim a bit better, I imagine that we'll have a better chance of finding out who killed him."

I took the dogs and returned to my cottage to freshen up. I'd just poured a glass of iced tea when my cell phone rang. It was Parker. "Hey, Parker. Any word on Deborah Goldfield?"

"She woke up and seems fairly coherent."

I opened the screen door and stepped onto the deck. "That's such good news."

"She doesn't remember the assault and can't identify her attacker, but she did remember picking up her husband's ashes. Deborah was glad they were safe since when she was told that she hadn't had a purse or any ID on her when she'd been found, she assumed the mugger got them as well as her wallet."

In a way, I supposed it worked out well that she had forgotten the ashes on the bus.

"Did she say what I should do with the ashes?"

Parker replied. "She asked if you could hang onto them. She'll be in the hospital for observation for a few more days due to her age. Her friend, Glorene, plans to pick her up when she's released and bring her home. Deborah indicated that she had your cell phone number from the message you left on her voicemail, and if it was okay with you, she'd call you when she returned to Gooseberry Bay, and you could drop the ashes off at her home."

"That's fine. The urn containing Deborah's husband's ashes is in my safe. They'll be safe until she can receive them."

I figured I'd call Romy Mansfield once I hung up with Parker, and then I could consider this case closed. I just hoped the situations Justice and Phoenix presented could be solved as easily.

Chapter 6

While I enjoyed the time I'd spent with the dogs as we lounged on the deck of my cottage overlooking the bay, my mind was restless at the same time. The situation with Riley had left me feeling extremely unsettled, but Justice's situation terrified me. Based on everything I'd heard, it really sounded like the boy might be guilty.

Rather than calling Adam for an update, I'd initially decided to wait for Adam to reach out to me, but waiting for news was making me crazy, so eventually, I decided to reverse my original decision and make the call.

"Adam?" I asked when he answered in a voice so defeated that it didn't sound like him.

"Hey, Ainsley. I was thinking about giving you a call."

I could hear traffic in the background, which didn't seem right. "Are you at the academy?"

"No. I'm sitting in my car in front of the police station."

My heart sank. "Police station? I thought Dani interviewed Justice and let him go."

"She did," Adam confirmed. "But since there have been some new developments, she wanted to speak to me alone, so I left Justice with Archie and came into town."

"New developments?" I asked, bracing myself for the worst.

Adam took a moment before he answered. "Dani has been doing some research, and it seems that she was able to dig up the likely reason Justice was so enraged when he saw Clark Oberson at the baseball game on Tuesday. Apparently, Oberson was a teacher at the high school Justice's sister, Lydia, attended when she was murdered."

Oh, this didn't sound good.

Adam continued. "At the time of Lydia's murder, it was Justice's contention that it was Oberson and not Lydia's boyfriend, Roger, who killed her. In his report, the detective who interviewed Justice stated that Justice insisted that Lydia died while trying to protect a friend."

"Protect a friend, how?"

"According to what Justice told the detective at the time of the murder, Lydia knew that her best friend, Collette Johnson, who was a junior at the same high school Lydia attended, had been seduced by Oberson. Also, according to Justice, when Lydia heard about the affair, she threatened to tell the authorities. Based on the statements made by Justice during the interview, Oberson was interviewed, but he denied everything. Collette was also interviewed and was, in fact, asked point blank if she'd been sleeping with her teacher, but, like Oberson, she denied everything. Based on the interviews with Oberson and Collette, it sounds like Oberson was never considered a viable suspect. At least not by the police, although based on comments made by Justice on Tuesday, in Justice's mind, the guy killed his sister and got away with it."

"Which gives Justice a motive and provides Dani with a reason to suspect him of the murder."

"It does," Adam agreed. "I guess there was a witness to the verbal altercation between Justice and Oberson, and the witness told Dani that Justice threatened to even the score."

"That really does sound bad."

Adam sighed. "It is bad. And there's one more thing that makes it even worse."

At this point, the only thing I could do was to brace myself for the bad news.

"Clark Oberson was strangled, and his body was found under the bleachers at the high school, which you know since you are the one to have found him.

What you may not know is that Justice's sister, Lydia, was strangled, and her remains were likewise found under the bleachers at the high school she attended at the time of her death."

I had heard that, but Adam might not have known that, and I didn't suppose it mattered at this point. "So two years ago, Justice's sister, Lydia, was murdered, and Justice believes it was a teacher at her school, Oberson, who killed her. He has no proof, and Oberson denies it and seems to get away with it, but then Oberson shows up here in Gooseberry Bay a few days ago, and Justice goes berserk and kills the guy to avenge his sister's death."

"That's the theory Dani is going with. She wanted to speak to me about it first, and she was nice enough to allow me to bring Justice in rather than sending her team up to the academy to arrest him in front of his teachers and fellow students."

I supposed that was nice of her, especially since it sounded like Justice might be guilty.

"Does Dani have any other suspects?"

"Not that she's shared with me. I have to admit this appears to be bad. Really bad."

I felt so bad for Adam. I could hear the stress in his voice. "So what are you going to do?"

"Right now, I'm going to return to the academy to pick Justice up and bring him down to the station for booking. I don't want to do this, but I don't have a choice. I do think it will be easier on Justice if I bring him in as opposed to him being arrested by uniformed officers. Once that's done, I guess I'll regroup and try to figure out my next move."

"I'm here for you if you want to come by."

"I appreciate that, but I think I should be with the staff and students at the academy tonight. They'll likely have questions and the need to process everything. At this point, my plan is to pick Justice up, bring him into town, and then head home. I will call you later and let you know how things went."

"Okay. I guess that would be best. I love you."

"I love you, too."

With that, he hung up.

I took a moment to process things before I called the dogs and returned to Jemma's. I understood why Adam felt he needed to be with his staff and the boys who lived at the academy tonight, but that didn't mean the rest of the peninsula gang couldn't put our heads together and try to find a way out of this mess.

"What's wrong?" Jemma asked the moment I walked into her cottage through the front door.

"I just spoke to Adam. It's bad." I shared the content of our conversation.

"Wow. That does sound pretty bad," Jemma agreed with my assessment of the situation. "How old is Justice?"

"Fifteen, so he's a minor, but given the circumstances, it seems possible he'll be tried as an adult if it goes that far."

"Do you think it will go that far?"

"I don't know. Justice seems to have had a motive to kill Oberson, and he did take off last night. Even though it looks pretty bad, I'm still hoping this is one of those 'it's the darkest before the dawn moments,' and everything works out fine."

Jemma shot me a look of sympathy. "How did Adam sound when you spoke to him?"

"Tired. Stressed. I guess it would be accurate to say that Adam was somewhat deflated. You have to admit that things are looking pretty hopeless."

"I guess they are. The guy had only been in town for a couple of days before he was murdered. That isn't a lot of time to make new enemies, so it seems likely that whoever killed him is a shadow from his past."

Jemma's cell phone dinged. She picked it up and looked at the screen. "It's a text from Parker, letting me know that she's coming over on the five o'clock ferry and will be here for the weekend."

"That's great," I said. "Parker will likely have a lot of good input about the Justice situation."

"And the Phoenix situation, which I will bring you up to speed on in a minute." She began to type in a reply. "I'm going to invite her to dinner. If Josie doesn't want to cook, we'll order in."

Once she'd sent the text, she returned her attention to me.

"So what about the Phoenix situation?" I asked, curious as to what Jemma might have come up with.

Jemma got up from the table, where she'd been working on her laptop, and walked into the kitchen. She grabbed a soda and offered me one, but I declined. Jemma then headed over to the sofa, scooted Stefan aside, and sat down. "It seems as though Phoenix might have been onto something when she told you things felt off. As far as I can tell, Ralston Richardson from Panguitch, Utah, doesn't exist. I know Phoenix said he'd told her he hadn't lived there long, and that might be the case. Perhaps he never really established his residency there by updating his driver's license, opening a bank account, registering with the post office, or entering into gainful employment, but if he wasn't there long enough to do any of those things, which would explain the lack of a link to the town, why even mention it? Why not just say he was from the last place he had established himself as a resident?"

"Good question. What about the truck Ralston drives now? When Phoenix sent the text with the plate number, she mentioned that the truck had Utah plates."

"The truck is registered to Merlin Gibbins. Mr. Gibbins last lived in Moab, Utah, but he passed away last January. It's unclear at this point why Ralston Richardson is driving the dead man's truck, but my initial thought was that he stole it, so I looked for a police report involving a stolen truck matching the one Ralston is driving, but there isn't a match."

"I suppose Gibbins might have been a friend or neighbor who lent it to him or even gave it to him before he died."

"Perhaps."

"Anything else?"

"Unfortunately, I didn't find a lot, which is concerning in and of itself. I'm good at what I do, and if I couldn't find anything related to a geologist named Ralston Richardson, then it's likely because the guy doesn't exist."

I sat back in my chair. "Okay, so if we can't find anything related to anyone with the name and background the guy is currently using, and the truck he's driving is registered to a dead man, what do we do next?"

Jemma replied. "The truck still seems like a lead to me. Merlin Gibbons was married, and as far as I can tell, his widow still lives in the same house she lived in with him. I'd start by speaking to her. She may have the rest of the story about the truck and might even know the name of the man her husband lent it to, assuming that's even what happened. I suppose it's possible that Gibbons sold it to Ralston, but the man never followed up and changed the title with the DMV."

"Speaking to the wife of the man the truck is registered to is a good idea. Do you have a phone number for her?"

"I do," she rattled off the number. "If that lead doesn't pan out, we might need to consider having Phoenix do a little recon."

"Recon?" I asked.

"Maybe have her go through Ralston's wallet while he's in the shower or otherwise indisposed. We know he doesn't have a driver's license from Washington State under the name Ralston Richardson, but he may have a license in his wallet from another state or a license with another name on it. He may also have credit cards bearing another name. It would be worth looking."

"That sounds dangerous."

"Not if she does it right."

"Perhaps she can get something of his with his DNA on it while she's snooping around. And maybe I can show her how to pull a print. The first step really does seem to be to ID the guy."

"That would give us a place to start. We can talk more about involving Phoenix if all else fails, but one of my other ideas might pan out, and we won't need to involve her at all."

Josie wandered in just then, and the subject of conversation naturally transitioned from Phoenix and her problem to Justice and his.

"I take it you heard?" I asked Josie.

"I heard. Everyone at the academy is totally freaking out. Adam called and spoke to Archie after he spoke to Dani, and then Archie filled Hudson, Andi, and me in. To say we were shocked that Justice was actually going to be arrested for killing that teacher is putting it mildly. Archie got on the phone with the Winchester attorney, who, as you might suspect, is one of the best attorney's money can buy.

He doesn't specialize in criminal law but knows enough about the subject to act on Justice's behalf during the booking process. If it looks as if this mess isn't going to get cleared up as quickly as everyone hopes, he'll refer the case to a colleague who specializes in criminal defense."

The idea that Justice needed the services of a criminal defense attorney had my stomach tied up in knots.

"Did you stay until Adam arrived to take Justice into town?" Jemma asked.

"I stayed until Adam arrived to speak to Justice, but I didn't sit in on the conversation. Once Adam left with Justice, Hudson, Andi, and Archie called all the boys into the dining hall to fill them in. I was going to stay, but it felt like a family moment, so I decided to return to the cottage and wait with you all." She took a deep breath. "On the one hand, everyone is worried that Dani won't be able to find the evidence needed to clear Justice." Josie paused. "On the other hand, however, I think there is an idea out there that Justice did do it, which has caused an equal amount of worry that Dani will find the proof needed to send him away for a very long time."

"If he did it, then he should face the consequences of his actions," Jemma pointed out.

"I guess," Josie agreed.

I felt so bad for Josie. I knew Justice pretty well since I was spending a fair amount of time at the academy with Adam now that we were officially dating, but I didn't hang out with the boys like Josie did. While I could say Justice and I were casual acquaintances, Josie and Justice seemed to be friends.

Coop wandered in with his dog, Hank. Even though Hank was almost completely blind, he was familiar with Jemma and Josie's cottage and managed to get around without running into anything. Whenever he arrived, he always liked to get a lay of the land, so he greeted Kai and Kallie and then made his way around the room to greet each person. Once Hank had said hi to everyone and settled in on the large dog pillow near the fireplace, which everyone knew was his, Coop asked for an update, and Josie and I took a few minutes to fill him in.

Coop seemed to be intently listening as we filled him in. The man had a quiet and deliberate way about him that I recognized as his way of processing essential information. He wasn't usually quick to share his ideas, but when he did, they were usually worth listening to.

Eventually, he spoke. "My initial thought as you were sharing the details of the past few days was that it was likely significant that both Lydia James and Clark Oberson were killed in the same manner and left in the same setting. On the surface, it creates a link between them. One might assume that Justice killed Oberson and then intently posed him under the bleachers in the same manner Oberson posed Lydia, but one might also conclude that a single individual killed them both." He paused and then continued. "My hunch, however, is that we have a copycat. Someone who wanted to kill Oberson knew the details of Lydia's death, knew that Justice and

Oberson argued, and knew that Justice would be seen as a viable suspect."

"So, the method used to kill the man and the location of the body dump were both intentionally orchestrated to create a link between Justice and Oberson's death," I said.

"That would be my guess," Coop confirmed.

A frame would make sense. Of course, the frame wouldn't have worked had Justice not left the academy last night, which most likely meant that not only did Oberson's killer know about Lydia but also knew that Justice was in town and not at the academy, where he would have had an alibi. Had someone contacted Justice and prompted him to leave the safety of his room to head into town? Or had the person who killed Oberson, assuming it wasn't Justice, simply seen him in town and decided to use Justice's volatile mental state to kill Oberson and pin it on the grieving brother who had every reason to want the man dead?

"So what do we do now?" Josie asked. "How do we help Justice?"

"How do we help Justice do what?" Parker asked as she breezed in through the front door just as Josie had voiced her question.

As a group, we went through the whole thing again for Parker's sake. I was glad Parker was here. As a crime reporter for a major newspaper, she had connections the rest of us didn't have. She also had a sleuth-like way of looking at things that I'd found invaluable when working on cases in the past.

Actually, between my investigation skills, Jemma's computer know-how, Parker's contacts and logical thinking, Coop's muscle, and Josie's natural ability to get people to talk even if they had reason not to, the peninsula gang made a pretty good team. The only person who could have made the team better was my FBI sister, who had gone off on a mission a month ago and had yet to return.

"Since I have spaghetti sauce in the freezer, I'm going to heat it, prepare some pasta, and toss together a salad; then we can chat while we eat," Josie said. "If you want to continue to chat while I cook, I can hear from the kitchen."

Josie got up and headed to the kitchen, and I decided to join her. It didn't seem right that she'd have to make the meal without help. I could put together a salad and maybe butter some bread to heat in the oven.

"I'm worried about Adam," I said as I pulled lettuce, tomatoes, and other fixings for the salad from the refrigerator.

"Yeah. Me too," Josie agreed. "In fact, I'm worried about everyone at the academy. Justice has had his issues since he's been there, and I definitely wouldn't go so far as to say that he's been an easy student for the staff or a likely friend for the other boys, but he is family. I think everyone will experience big feelings about what has occurred and what might happen in the future."

It didn't take long to prepare the meal, and it seemed there was a general agreement not to discuss anything with an intensely emotional charge while we ate. Jemma shared that she'd spoken to Hope today and that Hope had been putting pressure on her to chair the annual Halloween event sponsored by the community. Jemma had a flexible schedule and likely had the time to make that sort of commitment, but she wasn't sure she wanted to take on such a huge task, and, to tell you the truth, I didn't blame her.

Once the subject of community events had been exhausted, Coop shared the highlights of the fascinating air charter he'd been busy with this afternoon. I had to admit that Coop had a lot of interesting stories to tell. Based on my observations, it sounded more than likely that the individuals who chartered a private chopper to get around lived lives that were much more interesting than the general population.

Once the meal was consumed, Jemma did the dishes while the rest of us focused our energy, intent on devising a stellar plan.

"Maybe there are clues to be found in Clark Oberson's residence," I said. "It's not that I'm excited about adding breaking and entering to my resume, but even though I'm fairly sure law enforcement has already searched the place, sometimes the police miss things. Especially the little things that can often make all the difference in the story we're trying to tell."

"Checking out his residence is a good idea," Parker said. "I can use my contacts to get an address, and you and I will go tomorrow."

One of the reasons why Parker was so good at what she did was because she was decisive and willing to take risks.

"What time do you want to leave?" I asked.

"Not too early since our presence is more apt to appear suspicious to anyone who might notice us if we're in the area before breakfast. Maybe around ten. Since I have no food in my cottage, maybe we can meet for breakfast at nine and head to the property, which I'm confident I will have identified by then."

"That sounds good to me," I confirmed.

Parker stood up. "I know it's still early, but I have an article to finish writing and send in before I can start my weekend." She looked at me and said. "I'll see you at nine." Then she scanned the room and said. "And I'll see the rest of you sometime after that."

After she left, I chatted with the others for a little longer, and then the dogs and I headed out for a short walk before settling into my cottage for the night. Once I'd made a cup of tea and changed into my most comfortable pajamas, I'd gathered my thoughts sufficiently to text Adam, letting him know I was available to talk if he wanted to. I made it clear, however, that there wouldn't be any hard feelings if the timing wasn't good, and he preferred to wait to call until the following day. If I knew Adam, which I did, I was sure he had taken on everyone's worry and grief, which meant he likely wouldn't have much energy left to deal with his own.

Since I wasn't expecting him to call, I was startled when my cell phone rang soon after the text was sent. It wasn't Adam but Phoenix.

"Hey, Phoenix. Is everything okay?"

"Everything is the same. After getting your text about meeting tomorrow to discuss ways to find out more about my mom's new boyfriend, it occurred to me that he might have a driver's license or credit card in his wallet with a name other than Ralston Richardson. He took his wallet out to pay for pizza and left it on the coffee table after he paid. He went into the bedroom with my mother, so I figured they'd be awhile and decided to take a peek."

"And what did you find?"

"He has four credit cards in four different names."

"Can you text the names to me?"

"I can."

"And the driver's license?"

"It was issued to a man from Santa Fe, New Mexico named Keith Hilton. The photo looks like Ralston, but the other information, including the age of the license holder, is wrong."

"So it's likely a fake."

"That was my impression."

"Take photos of everything and then put them back. Go to your room and hang out there. It will be best for you to avoid the guy. I've found that sometimes the guilty look on our faces after we've been snooping can give us away, even if we don't think we have anything to be guilty about."

Phoenix promised to do as I asked, and then she hung up to follow my instructions. I promised to talk to her on the phone and meet with her tomorrow afternoon. She expressed her gratitude that I'd taken her gut instinct seriously, and I assured her that I'd always be there for her no matter what.

Chapter 7

Adam texted me back last night to let me know he was tied up with the boys but would call me this morning. He didn't say what time, so I confirmed I had my cell phone in my pocket before I took the dogs for a walk. Parker had indicated that we should meet at nine for breakfast, which sounded good since I was hungry, but I didn't think a public restaurant was the best place for us to chat, so I suggested that she just come over to my cottage and I'd make breakfast for us. I had eggs, whole grain bread from the bakery, fresh spinach, cheese, and passable mushrooms, so I figured I could put a tasty meal together.

The dogs seemed disappointed that we weren't taking a longer walk this morning, which I felt conflicted about, but since I still needed to shower and dress, a longer walk would have to wait. Once I'd showered and changed clothes, I headed to the kitchen and began to pull the ingredients I needed for our breakfast out of the refrigerator. Adam called as I was washing the spinach.

"Hey," I answered. "Thanks for calling. How are things?"

"As well as can be expected, I suppose."

The poor guy sounded exhausted.

He continued. "The arraignment is this morning, and our attorney is working on a deal to allow Justice to be released on bail into my custody. Since the entire case against Justice is circumstantial and related to the argument between Justice and Oberson, he believes he can accomplish this. Justice did say something about Oberson not getting away with it during that argument, which I will admit will be hard to get around. Our attorney said that Justice might be considered a flight risk, which could prevent the judge from allowing him out on bail. But since Justice doesn't have a car, a passport, or even a driver's license, and he doesn't have a lot of cash on hand, our attorney felt that we could mitigate that with the right supervision."

"I guess they could use an ankle monitor if they're overly concerned that he'll take off."

"He won't like that, but I'm sure he'll think it preferable to being locked up in a jail cell while this all gets straightened out."

Adam didn't have long to chat since he needed to meet with the attorney before the arraignment, so I wished him well and hung up. By the time the call ended, I could see Parker walking along the dirt pathway that connected all the cottages one to another. The veggies were washed, and the eggs whipped and ready to be cooked, so I was all set to start preparing our meal when she wanted to eat.

"Are omelets okay for breakfast?" I asked.

"That sounds perfect. I'm starving."

I turned the stovetop on to heat the pan. "By the way, before we get into our investigation of Oberson, remember I mentioned to you last night that I planned to contact the wife of the deceased man the truck Ralston is driving is registered to."

"I remember."

"I managed to connect with the wife, who told me that she gave the truck to Ralston in exchange for doing some work around her home for her. Heavy work like building a chicken coop and tilling the garden. She also said he assured her he would register it in his name, but it appears he never did."

"If I had to guess, the guy never intended to register it."

"I guess he probably didn't," I agreed. "I'm not sure how relevant it even is that he's driving a truck registered to a dead man, but it seemed to be worth mentioning. Were you able to get your article turned in on time?" I was really just making small talk, but it seemed more appropriate to do so than to jump right into a discussion relating to Justice and the tragic murder that would likely be felt throughout the community even though the victim had only recently arrived in our small town.

"I was. I called Alfred to let him know the article was finished and told him about the murder in Gooseberry Bay, so now I'm officially on that story." Parker referred to Alfred Sutton, her boss and crime reporter for the *Seattle News*.

"Even though you were supposed to have the weekend off?"

She shrugged. "It's okay, and it makes sense that Alfred would assign the story to me since I was already here, and this is my home territory. Snooping around in the official capacity as the crime reporter for the *Seattle News* will make things easier."

It was true that Parker acting officially on behalf of the newspaper would open some doors that might otherwise remain closed.

I slid the omelets onto the plates after they'd turned a golden color. I had toast warming in the oven, so I grabbed it, too. I refilled both my coffee cup and the cup Parker had helped herself to when she'd walked in, and then once we were settled, I asked Parker if she'd had any new ideas since the previous evening. She said she wasn't sure how accurate her intel was, but she was looking into a few things and hoped to hear back shortly. "In the meantime, we'll eat before heading to the motel as planned."

"Oberson was living in a motel?" I asked. The last I'd heard, Parker had planned to use her connections to locate his residence, but I'd never heard whether or not she was successful.

"Yes, I'm sorry. I thought I already mentioned that. I called Ryker, and he discovered that Oberson had been staying in the extended stay motel on the north end of town since he arrived for his substitute teaching gig."

"I guess a motel makes sense since he was only supposed to be in town until school let out for the summer. Did you get a room number?"

"Unit 2D. I figured we'd scoot over there, look around a little bit, and get out before anyone notices us."

"Do you have a key?"

"I have something even better." She held up a lock-picking kit.

"I'm going to pretend that's a key and that we have permission to look around," I said, preferring to live in denial than to admit that I was actually planning to commit a crime.

I just rinsed the dishes and stacked them in the sink. I figured I could take the time to wash them when I got back, assuming I wasn't in jail for breaking and entering. I'd already arranged for Kai and Kallie to hang out with Jemma and the cats, so I called them to come with me, and then we followed Parker out the front door. The drive to the motel was only about a ten-minute trip. When we arrived, we found the parking lot mostly empty, but thankfully, there was a car in the circle in front of the motel office, which likely would mean that the desk clerk would be tied up. Parker parked around back, and then we hurried up the stairs to the second floor. Unit 2D was on the end farthest away from the office, which was fortunate as well.

Once Parker did her thing, we slipped into the room, shutting the door behind us. There was little doubt that the guy was probably a slob since there were clothes strewn everywhere. Of course, the strewn clothing might indicate that someone, maybe even the police, had already searched the room. It would make sense that looking for clues as to what had occurred would be one of the first things Deputy Dani Dixon would have done.

"You go through the closet and dresser, and I'll begin sorting through the mess on the bed and floor," Parker suggested.

I did as Parker instructed, but I didn't find a lot. A few items of clothing that hadn't ended up on the floor, an empty suitcase, and a binder with notes left for the substitute from the teacher out on maternity leave. A takeout bag from the Chinese restaurant was tucked into the corner of the closet behind the suitcase. There was clothing piled atop the bag, effectively hiding it unless you thoroughly searched the closet. That seemed odd since if it had been me who'd ordered takeout, I would have tossed the bag in the trash can when I was done with it rather than stashing it on the floor of the closet behind a solid object. Once I picked the bag up, I carefully opened it, uncertain if I even wanted to know what I would find inside it.

"I think I have something," I said after I stepped out of the closet and back into the room.

"What did you find?"

"A takeout bag with money inside."

"How much money?"

"A lot."

Parker walked toward me. After she looked inside the bag, she said, "I guess we should give this to Dani."

"And how will we give this to Dani without mentioning that we broke into the room in the first place?"

Parker shrugged. "We'll wing it. Did you find anything else?"

"No. Did you?"

"A deck of cards on the table next to the bed. It's a new deck that hasn't even been opened, so I doubt it will provide a clue, but I'm taking it with me anyway." She held up a poker chip. "I also found this under the bed. It was tucked between the carpet and the wall at the head of the bed. If I hadn't really been looking, I wouldn't have noticed it."

I frowned. "It's a regular blue poker chip. The kind that lots of people use for poker night with their friends. How is that a clue?"

She shrugged once again. "Like the cards, it's likely to get us nowhere, but there's no harm in taking it with us."

A deck of cards and a regular blue poker chip didn't seem like real clues, but a bag of money might be.

"I'm going to dust for prints in the bathroom before we go," I said. "I'm not sure we'll find anything helpful since the murder didn't occur in the room, so there's no reason to believe the killer was ever in the room, but, like the cards and the poker chip, it doesn't hurt to grab what we can."

"I'm heading to the car to call Dani about the money. Meet me down there."

I quickly dusted for prints from the areas around the sink and toilet, and then I scurried down to meet Parker. She informed me that Dani was on her way. Parker had made Dani promise that anything we told her during the conversation would be considered to include immunity for both her and me regarding the method of accessing the clues we planned to turn over, and Dani had agreed. While I didn't know the new deputy all that well, Parker trusted her, and since Parker wasn't the sort to trust many people, I decided not to worry about the breaking and entering part of our exploit.

"You said you found this money in Clark Oberson's room?" Dani asked Parker.

"Ainsley found it in the closet."

Dani frowned. "I already had my men process the room, and neither mentioned finding any money."

"It was pretty well hidden," I said, attempting to cover for the deputies, who seemed to have messed up big time.

"If I know the men I sent, they likely opened the closet door, poked their heads inside, and considered it processed."

"If these guys are this sloppy regularly, why not fire them?" I asked.

Dani looked at me. "Hiring and firing is not my call. While things are better and the corruption factor has been minimized now that Deputy Todd is gone, I'm afraid that many of the problems in the department haven't been solved yet." She held the bag up. "Thanks for calling me about the cash. I'll do my best to track down the source. If I can do that, then perhaps I'll be able to find a suspect other than Justice."

"Are you actively trying to do that?" I asked. "Find a suspect other than Justice?"

"I am. I hated having to arrest the kid, but, like I said, I'm not the one making all the calls. After he was brought in, Justice and I sat down and had a rather long conversation. In my opinion, the kid is innocent, but the sheriff disagrees with me. He thinks he has adequate cause to arrest the kid, and he has more pull with the DA than I do, so if Justice is going to get a fair shake, we will need to find the real killer."

With that, she left, and I let out the metaphorical breath I had held ever since this breaking-and-entering game had begun.

"So what now?" I asked Parker.

"Let's head back to the peninsula and regroup. While the cards and the poker chip might eventually come in handy, they don't provide us with an immediate avenue of investigation."

"I need to talk to Jemma about some things Phoenix shared with me last evening, too. I'll catch you up while I'm at it."

Chapter 8

After Parker and I greeted the dogs and cats, we poured ourselves cups of coffee before sitting at the dining table where Jemma had been working on her laptop when we arrived. In addition to the list of names Phoenix had found on the credit cards in Ralston's wallet, I'd also given Jemma the name on the driver's license, which appeared to have been a fake.

"Let's talk about the driver's license first," Jemma said to Parker and me once we were settled. "I found three Keith Hilton's living in New Mexico, but only one lives in Santa Fe. We know from what Phoenix has told us that the guy her mother is dating, who has a driver's license with his photo but the name Keith Hilton on it in his wallet, is likely in his thirties. The Keith Hilton I found in Santa Fe is sixty-two. But here's the thing, I dug around a bit and discovered that Keith Hilton has a son, Samuel. Samuel, who is thirty-two, took his mother's surname when his parents divorced. His mother's name was Joanna Richardson."

"Same last name as Ralston," I said.

Jemma nodded. "There's more. Joanna's father was named Ralston Richardson. Samuel's middle name is Ralston."

Parker jumped in. "So the guy practically living in Phoenix's house is likely Samuel Ralston Richardson, son of Keith Hilton and Joanna Richardson, and grandson to Ralston Richardson, who, for reasons unbeknownst to us at this point, has his father, Keith Hilton's, driver's license with his photo superimposed over the top of his father's photo."

"That appears to be the case," Jemma answered. "Lots of people go by their middle names, so the fact that he has presented himself as Ralston Richardson isn't all that alarming, but I have no idea why this man would be walking around with his father's driver's license."

"What, if anything, do you know about the father?" I asked.

Jemma leaned back in her chair. "Keith Hilton grew up in Nacogdoches, Texas. He was the middle of three children, all boys. The man was the unsettled sort who never finished high school but was a strong kid and managed to make a living doing physical labor on the ranches in the area. He eventually got a job as a long-haul truck driver. He did that for about fifteen years until he was arrested for killing a man in a bar fight. I was working on trying to figure out what he did after he got out of prison five years ago, but other than the fact that he has a driver's license from Santa Fe, New Mexico, I haven't been able to track him down. I'll keep trying."

"Okay," I said, taking a moment to process things and develop a mental timeline. "You said that Keith Hilton is sixty-two. He got out of prison five years ago when he was fifty-seven. He was in prison for fifteen years, which would have made him forty-two when he went in. For the sake of this conversation, let's say that the guy Phoenix's mom is dating is thirty-two. That would mean that his father was thirty when his son was born. Based on your research, what was Keith doing when he was thirty?"

Jemma looked down at her notes. "Even though I'd have to verify this, at this point, I'm going to say he was a truck driver."

"Was Keith married to the mother of his child?" Parker asked.

"I haven't gotten that far yet, but I'll find out. I started with the credit cards, which took up most of my time this morning, and had just gotten started on Keith Hilton when you walked in."

"So, what did you find out about the credit cards?" I asked.

"All were issued to men in different states who died within the past six months."

"So this guy finds out that some guy died, steals his card, and then uses it until someone eventually closes the account," Parker said. "That's fairly ingenious, actually. If the deceased man left a widow behind, chances are that she's too deeply entrenched in her mourning to take care of things like closing accounts. She likely merely pays the bill each month, intending to straighten everything out once she gets past the worst of her suffering. First, there is the shock and denial, and then there is the funeral to get through. Once that's behind her, she'll need to deal with the grief when reality sets in. Then there is the anger and the blame, and eventually the acceptance. This is typically the stage when the widow will begin to rebuild her life and when she may begin to notice things such as suspicious charges on the credit card. By this point, the credit card thief has moved onto another dead man and another credit card."

That sounded like a very likely scenario to me. Even if I hadn't been concerned about Phoenix, her mother, and her sibling's safety before, I would be now.

"So, what do we know about this guy?" Parker asked. "From the beginning."

I answered. "We know the guy showed up here in Gooseberry Bay a few months ago. Or at least he started dating Phoenix's mom a few months ago once her divorce was finalized. I suppose it's possible that he'd been in the area longer. Phoenix met him when she came home for spring break the first week of April. She said that the guy was not only better looking than most men she'd met but was younger than she'd expected he'd be. She didn't say how old he was, and I don't think she knows for sure, but she is certain he's younger than her mother. She also said that it was obvious that Riley, who just turned eighteen, had a little crush on him. He seemed only to have eyes for the mother and treated Riley in a manner that seemed to be appropriate for the situation, so Phoenix wasn't overly worried about it. Then she came home last week and noticed that Riley's crush had grown into infatuation, and this is when she decided to do a background check. As you are aware, she found a lot of holes, which is when she decided to talk to me. I did a preliminary search and found a lack of a paper trail alarming enough to warrant a deeper search. Phoenix managed to look in his wallet while he was in the bedroom with her mother, and she found the fake driver's license and the stolen credit cards. I asked Jemma to look into things, and here we are."

"Anything else?" Parker asked.

"The guy told Phoenix's mother that he was a geologist, but Phoenix says he doesn't appear to know a thing about geology. She's sure he's lying, although she has no idea why he would lie about something like that, especially since her mother isn't dating him because of his job."

"The guy sounds like a pathological liar," Parker said. "Pathological liars don't need a reason to lie; they merely lie because they can't help it."

"He also told her mother that he was from Panguitch, Utah, but it can't be verified because there's no record of him living there. Phoenix said that he also told her he'd been a long-haul trucker at some point, and that career seemed to fit, so maybe he actually followed in his daddy's footsteps and learned to drive a truck."

"Do you believe this man is an immediate threat to Phoenix, her mother, or her siblings?" Parker asked.

"I'm not sure," I answered. "Phoenix didn't say anything to indicate as much. In fact, if not for Riley's crush, I doubt she would have even run the initial background check. She said the guy is nice and hasn't acted in a way that might be interpreted as inappropriate. Well, except for the fake ID and the stolen credit cards. Phoenix and I planned to get together once I got back from my errand with you. Maybe we should have her come over here instead."

Everyone agreed that was a good idea, so I called Phoenix, and she said she'd be by in about an hour. She would have come right away, but Riley was at school, and the babysitter her mother had hired for her preschool-aged siblings hadn't shown up yet, so she had to watch her younger siblings until the babysitter arrived.

"Ask Phoenix if she knows where Ralston lives," Parker said in the background.

I turned to her and held up a finger to let her know I'd respond momentarily. I then hung up with Phoenix and responded. "I asked her if she knew where he lived yesterday, but she said she didn't. She said her mother should know, but she wasn't sure how to ask her without it sounding odd."

"Maybe I can find something," Jemma said. "I'll just search for lodging transactions associated with the four cards the guy's carrying around in his wallet. He must be using one of them to pay his rent."

Jemma went to work on the computer, Parker went into the kitchen to scrounge for food, and I took the dogs for a short walk. I wanted to call Adam to see how things were going, but the odds were that he was still at the arraignment, or if the arraignment was over, he may have been processing things with his attorney. I thought about the money we found in Oberson's hotel room. To me, that seemed to indicate that he was into something illegal. Something that had gotten him killed. I knew Dani was looking into things, but I still felt I should be doing something more to help. What it was that I should be doing, I hadn't a clue, but I wasn't used to waiting it out on the sidelines.

Kai picked up a stick and brought it to me. I tossed it down the beach and waited for him to retrieve it. Kallie wasn't a fan of fetch. She'd go after a stick if I told her to since she was the sort to always want to please me, but she was just as happy to sit in the shade and watch Kai run back and forth along the beach. Because Kallie tended to be a lower-energy dog, keeping an eye on her weight was essential. She wasn't fat by any means, but a large dog like Kallie needed to maintain an optimum weight if I didn't want her to suffer from a strain being placed on her joints.

When I returned to the cottage, Jemma was chatting with Parker about the charges on the credit card assigned to Jeff Dorchester for Ralston's rent. Based on the charges, it appeared that Ralston Richardson had shown up here in Gooseberry Bay around the first of March and had been staying in the studio apartment ever since. Jemma then hacked into the financial records for the apartment complex and found that the apartment that had been paid for by Jeff Dorchester had been rented out to a man named Keith Hilton. I guess that made sense. Ralston would have shown the complex manager his driver's license if he had asked for an ID. I couldn't help but wonder why the complex manager hadn't questioned why Hilton was using a credit card issued to someone other than him, but maybe he either didn't notice or didn't care.

Phoenix arrived just as Parker and I prepared to leave to check out the apartment Jemma had identified. I thought it would be best if Phoenix waited with Jemma, so I suggested that they work together to dig up new leads while Parker and I did a little recon.

Parker and I headed across town and parked across the street from the small apartment complex. We discussed the idea of approaching the apartment and knocking on the door. Ralston didn't know either of us, so we could merely say we had the wrong apartment if he answered, and if he didn't answer, we could assume that Ralston had left for the day and take the opportunity to break in and snoop around a bit. We were still discussing the pros and cons when a handsome man with jet-black hair came out of the apartment and headed toward his truck.

"That's Ralston," Parker said. "I recognize him from his fake driver's license."

"Should we wait until he leaves and let ourselves in?"

"No. We can break in anytime. Let's follow the guy and see where he goes."

Ralston pulled out of the parking lot and headed north along the main highway that hugged the bay. Parker hung back just a bit so we wouldn't be spotted, but between the two of us, we didn't have all that hard of a time keeping an eye on the guy. After heading north for about ten minutes, he veered left and merged onto the main highway that led toward the westernmost coast of the peninsula.

"Where do you think he's going?" I asked.

"No idea," Parker responded. "But he doesn't appear to be in a hurry. In fact, he's actually driving five miles an hour under the speed limit, which makes it twice as hard to follow him without being seen."

"Maybe he has seen us and is leading us on a wild goose chase," I said.

"Maybe."

Parker slowed even more as the guy turned onto a dirt road. The road was well-groomed, so I assumed the fire department or one of the utility companies maintained it.

"If we turn onto this road, he'll make us for sure," I pointed out.

"Yeah. I'm going to continue driving down the road. If the guy turned onto the dirt road in an attempt to confirm his suspicion that we were following him, the worst thing we can do at this point is to follow him. I will admit that I'm curious, but we don't have guns or any other means of defense, and we really have no idea whether Ralston is carrying or not."

Parker continued driving down the road. Once she found a heavily forested place to pull over, she tucked the car behind a grove of trees, and we waited. We figured that if Ralston had been trying to lose us, he might have continued in the direction he'd been heading after he saw us pass him. We waited thirty minutes, but he never passed by, so we returned to the highway.

"I'm tempted to check out the dirt road now, but we have no way of knowing whether the guy headed back to town or is still there waiting for us to check things out," Parker said. "I guess we should head back to town and then come back to check it out later."

That sounded like a decent plan to me.

When we drove past Ralston's apartment, we noticed his truck was parked in the lot. He either completed the errand he set out to do or realized we were following him and decided to leave the task he'd set out to perform for another day.

"Now that we know Ralston is home, I guess we can go and check out the dirt road," I suggested.

Parker executed a perfect U-turn, and we were headed back to where we'd just come from. When we arrived at the dirt road, we turned onto it. Scanning the landscape as we drove, we looked for anything that might explain why Ralston might have come this way in the first place.

"There isn't anything other than a lot of nothing out here," I said. "Even if we do happen across the spot where Ralston was heading, how on earth are we even going to know it if we don't know what we're looking for."

Parker pointed down to the road to the left. "There. That looks like an old hunting shed. Let's take a look."

Once we arrived at the shed, we found a handwritten note on the door.

Better luck next time.

Chapter 9

By the time Parker and I returned to the roommates' cottage, Josie had returned from town, where she'd been attending a meeting with Hope about the upcoming summer events. Since Josie hoped to score the permit that would allow her to be the official food vendor for the Movies on the Beach event, Hope had asked her to present a proposal to the event committee.

"So, how did it go?" I asked. I knew how important this was to Josie.

"I think it went well," Josie replied. "The committee plans to look at all the proposals presented to them before making a decision, which makes sense. The committee liked my ideas, and since I've logged thousands of volunteer hours in the community, I think the group, as a whole, would prefer to go with a local who has put in their time."

"I'm sure the committee knows a good thing when they see it," Jemma said in support of her friend.

"I hope so," Josie replied.

Jemma looked at me. "So, how did the recon go?"

Parker jumped in with some very unladylike expletives. Parker wasn't the sort who enjoyed the experience of someone getting a leg up on her and had been upset since she'd seen the note, but even though I really was convinced the guy was up to no good, I couldn't help but laugh at his rather bold message to us. I mean, he could have just shot us, but he didn't. Instead, he left us a note that said, *Better luck next time*, but would most likely translate to, *I saw you. I know what you're after, and while I enjoyed the chase, I'm already one step ahead of you.*

"Maybe it's time to bring in the authorities," I suggested. "When all we had to go on was a feeling Phoenix had about the guy, going to the police wasn't really an option, but now we have the guy dead to rights on the use of a stolen identity and the stolen credit cards. The charges he'd made on Jeff Dorchester's credit card to pay for the apartment Ralston is staying in should be enough to get someone's attention."

"Dani is tied up with the Oberson murder case, but maybe I can call Ryker," Parker suggested. "When we chatted earlier, he told me he was off this weekend. He suggested the two of us should get together. Maybe he'd be willing to come here rather than getting together in Seattle."

"Do you really think he'll want to spend his weekend sleuthing?" Josie asked.

Parker shrugged. "He might be willing to if it means hanging out with all of us."

I knew she really meant that he might be willing to if it meant hanging out with her, but while everyone could see that Parker had a thing for the guy, she didn't seem to be willing to admit that what she had with Ryker was anything more than friendship quite yet.

"He can just sleep on my sofa," Parker added.

Josie let out an audible smirk, which caused Jemma to send her a look to remind her that Parker was fragile and it was best to tread lightly.

"I guess it wouldn't be the worst idea to call Ryker and ask him if he's interested in an all-expense paid trip to beautiful Gooseberry Bay," I responded.

"Coop is coming over after he gets back from his charter, so maybe we can grill tonight and discuss things. The dinner will give Coop and Ryker a chance to get to know each other better," Jemma suggested.

"And I can call and invite Adam," I added. "I'm not sure what the situation with Justice will look like by the end of the day, but I can call and invite him nonetheless."

"And I can likewise call and invite Hudson," Josie added. "Like Adam, he might be tied up, but I'm hoping that the judge let Justice out on bail, and things will calm down for a while."

"Have you heard anything about the arraignment?" I asked Josie.

"Not a word. Have you?"

I shook my head.

Parker called Agent Ryker while I called Adam. I'd been promising myself that I'd wait until Adam called me since I knew he was busy and hated to bother him, but by this point in the day, I'd had my fill of worry and truly needed to know what had happened.

"The judge wouldn't approve bail," Adam informed me. "He feels that Justice is a flight risk, and to be honest, I've been worried about that as well. Justice has lived on the street before. He has a comfort level with that sort of situation. Short of tying him up and locking him in his room, I wasn't sure how Archie and I were going to make him stay put."

"I'm so sorry, Adam. I know this has been a difficult time for you, and I can't begin to imagine how hard it's been on Justice and everyone at the academy."

"It has been. The one concession the judge was willing to make was to allow Justice to stay here in the two-cell Gooseberry Bay jail rather than having him transferred to county lockup as they normally would with an inmate staying longer than a single night. Dani has assured me that Archie, Hudson, and I can visit anytime we want, and she's fine with us bringing him items to make him comfortable, such as his handheld video game, some books, snacks, and even his cell phone. Of course, if he acts out or fails to comply with even one of the rules Dani plans to lay out, he can easily lose those privileges, but I think he'll cooperate. Justice isn't happy about the situation, but Dani is going out of her way to make him comfortable."

"I'm glad to hear that. Maybe letting Dani be the one to keep an eye on him while this gets straightened out isn't the worst idea."

"Maybe not."

"I'm sure you need to get back to what you were doing before I called, but the gang has another case we're working on related to Phoenix's mom's new boyfriend. It's a rather long story, and I can fill you in later, but we've found enough to ask Agent Dante Ryker to help, at least in an unofficial capacity."

"Unofficial capacity?"

"He's off duty this weekend, so he's coming to Gooseberry Bay as Parker's date. Well, sort of. I'll fill you in about that whole thing later as well. In the meantime, if you have some free time this evening, we're all getting together for a cookout at the roommates' cottage. Ryker should be here by six, so we'll likely begin to gather around then."

He hesitated before answering. "I'm not sure at this point how my evening will look. I miss you, and I could use some time to focus on something other than the situation with Justice, so an evening with the gang sounds pretty good right now. It might be worthwhile to discuss Justice's situation with Ryker. He might have some ideas about how to mitigate things moving forward." He paused and then continued. "I'll talk to Archie about it, and I'll come by if he's fine holding down the fort at the academy. I'll call and let you know either way."

We chatted for a few more minutes, and then Adam had to go. I went back to the others and filled them in on what I'd learned about Justice and the outcome of the arraignment. While we'd all been rooting for Justice to get out on bail, I think everyone in the group agreed that it really did seem likely that he would have taken off the first chance that he got, so maybe it was better that he stay where he was, at least for the time being.

Phoenix decided to pick Riley up from school. Riley usually rode the bus to and from school, but with everything we'd learned about Ralston, Phoenix felt better about giving her a ride. She planned to try to speak to her about the situation on the ride home. She doubted that Riley would listen to anything negative she had to say about Ralston. But Riley was an adult now, so maybe she'd matured to the point where she'd at least consider the facts Phoenix planned to present if she was careful about her method of presentation.

Josie needed to run to the store to pick up a few things for this evening's cookout, and Parker decided to go with her. She figured she should have more in the refrigerator than an expired bottle of ketchup and a box of baking soda if Ryker was spending the weekend at her cottage.

That left Jemma and me. I decided to take this opportunity to ask her what her gut instinct was telling her about the guy we'd spent the day investigating.

She paused before answering. "I'm not sure. The guy is definitely not the upstanding member of society he seems to be trying to present to the world, but I can't decide if there's more going on than just a fake ID and the stolen credit cards."

"Something more going on? Like what?" I asked.

She narrowed her gaze. "I'm not sure exactly. So far, I haven't dug up anything truly sinister about the guy, but I just have this feeling there might be something sinister to find."

"All the moving around, fake ID, stolen credit cards, and a lack of a personal history is concerning," I agreed. "The guy is good-looking and charming. He seems to draw in anyone he comes into contact with. He has all the makings of a con man or a serial killer. I'm hoping we're dealing with the first option, but I sense that your gut instinct has told you we might be dealing with the second scenario."

Jemma got up and crossed the room. "I don't know. I hope not. And I certainly don't have an ounce of proof to back up the idea that the guy has ever murdered anyone, let alone more than one someone, but the deeper I dig, the bigger the knot in my gut seems to get. There's just something about him. Not that I've ever met the guy in person, but even in the photos I dug up of him, the guy has that look."

I was fully aware of the specific sort of look Jemma was referring to. "I guess it's a good thing we're bringing Ryker in on things. If the guy is into something even worse than using a fake ID and stolen credit cards, we'll need to turn this whole thing over to the pros."

Jemma agreed.

"Part of me wants to shut my computer down and simply enjoy the rest of the weekend, but another part of me knows that I'm not going to be able to rest until I can put a finger on whatever it is that's causing me to feel the way I do," Jemma said.

"I can go and grab my computer. Two of us digging will double our chances of finding something."

"Actually, I'd appreciate that. Josie will be gone for at least ninety minutes. Let's see what we can dig up between now and then."

I'd just returned to Jemma's cottage with my computer and was preparing to log in when my cell phone rang, letting me know I had a call. I looked at the Caller ID and answered.

"Hey, Phoenix. What's up?"

"It's Riley. I'm at the school to pick her up, but when I got here, I was told that my mother's boyfriend already picked her up."

"They just let this guy take her?"

"She's eighteen, and she voluntarily went with him."

"Did you call her?"

"I did, but the call went straight to voicemail. I called the house and asked the babysitter if Riley was there to relieve her, and she said she hadn't arrived home from school yet. I'm going to head over to Ralston's apartment now."

"No, wait. Don't go alone. I'm on my way to pick you up at the high school. I'll be there in less than five minutes. Wait for me."

With that, I hung up and filled Jemma in. We both headed out to my SUV. I told her to call Parker and fill her in while I drove along the southern end of the bay and then up the hill to the high school. My mind insisted that the guy just took Riley out for yogurt, but my gut instinct told me otherwise.

Chapter 10

Jemma, Phoenix, and I went by Ralston's apartment, but he wasn't there. Not that we expected him to be, but I imagined we all hoped it would be that easy. Phoenix called the babysitter a second time to make sure Riley hadn't shown up since she'd called the first time, and then she called her mother. Phoenix's mother hadn't heard from Ralston or Riley, but she was sure there was no reason to worry. She suggested that Ralston might have decided to buy Riley the new shoes she'd been going on and on about having for graduation. Phoenix didn't want to get into the whole "boyfriend with a secret identity and serial killer vibe" thing over the phone, so at this point, she simply told her mother that it was important that she speak to Riley right away, and she asked her mother to try to contact Riley or Ralston directly. Her mother promised to call her daughter and her boyfriend, and then she hung up.

"If Riley doesn't call back in a few minutes, you're going to need to bring your mom up to speed," Jemma said to Phoenix as we headed back to the cottage to regroup.

"I know I need to talk to my mom about the fake ID and stolen credit cards, but my mom is totally into this guy. I'm uncertain whether or not I have sufficient evidence against the guy to convince her that her new love interest could pose a genuine threat to Riley."

"You're her daughter," I reminded her. "I'm sure she'll believe you over some guy she just met."

"Don't count on it," Phoenix groaned. "She's been different since the divorce. The divorce was amicable, but I think losing her marriage did a real number on her. She was so damaged until Ralston came along. She worships the guy. There was one time when I made a comment about it being odd that Ralston was so vague about not only his past but his current job, and my mom's response was to tell me that Ralston was the best thing to ever happen to her and I should mind my own business."

"If we don't find Riley soon, we'll make her listen," I said. "I really hope your mom is right about Riley and Ralston just being off buying shoes, but if that isn't the case, Riley could be in real trouble."

When Jemma and I finally arrived at the roommates' cottage after swinging by the high school for Phoenix to retrieve her car, Parker and Josie had returned from the store. After I suggested that we call the authorities, Parker pointed out that, at this time, we lacked a bona fide reason to contact law enforcement. All that had happened was that Ralston had picked Riley up from school, but even Phoenix had to admit this wouldn't be the first time he'd picked Riley or the younger kids up from school. Riley didn't know that Phoenix planned to pick her up, so she had no reason to wait for her, and she was an adult who had gone with him willingly. Riley's mother wasn't worried that her daughter had gone off with her boyfriend, and given the circumstances, the police wouldn't be concerned either. Yes, we did have the fake ID and the stolen credit cards, but for all we knew, Ralston had an explanation for all that.

"Okay, so what do we do if we can't contact Dani?" Jemma asked.

I looked at Phoenix, who had arrived a few minutes after Jemma and me, and saw a look of panic on her face. "Try calling Riley again. She didn't answer before, but maybe she will this time."

She didn't.

"How about friends?" I asked Phoenix. "If Riley had made plans with Ralston, is there anyone she might have told?"

"Stephie Boston or Ilia Rousten. Stephie is Riley's best friend of the moment, and Ilia has a tough home situation and tends to hang out at our house a lot."

"Do you have their numbers?"

She nodded.

"Call them and ask if they know where Riley is, but be casual. Just say something about her needing to get home to watch the younger kids," I instructed.

"Okay." Phoenix made the calls.

I could tell by what was being said on Phoenix's end that Stephie had no idea where Riley was, and Ilia didn't answer.

"Your mom mentioned shoes," I said to Phoenix after she hung up with Stephie. "Maybe Ralston did take Riley to buy shoes. I guess we can go and check out the shoe stores in town."

"That seems to be a waste of time," Phoenix said. "If Riley is buying shoes, she would have no reason to turn her cell phone off. The girl never turns her cell phone off."

I supposed Phoenix had a point.

"Are you sure the cell phone is turned off?" Jemma said. "Riley may just have silenced it, which explains why you got voicemail. It could still be on. If that's the case, maybe we can track it."

"Yeah, that's a good idea," Phoenix said. "My mom has everyone still living under her roof on a family tracker app. She wanted me to be on it, too, but I declined since I already had a different app on my phone. Why didn't I think of that."

"Can you get into the app? Do you have the password?" I asked.

"No, but if my mom truly thinks Riley is buying shoes, there's no reason for her not to look and verify that."

Phoenix called her mom back. She expressed her concern about Riley's whereabouts and eventually convinced her to check her app. According to the app, Riley was at the ferry terminal.

"Ferry terminal!" Phoenix screeched to her mother. "Why would Riley be waiting to catch a ferry?"

I couldn't hear the mother's response, but Phoenix hung up after less than a minute.

"What if Ralston has her and is making his escape?" Phoenix cried. "We need to get to her before the next ferry leaves."

"Ryker's coming in on the next ferry," Parker said. "I spoke to him a little while ago, and he caught an earlier ferry."

Jemma pulled the ferry schedule up on her computer. "The next ferry will dock at four-ten, which is in five minutes, and the next ferry to board and leave from our side of the Sound toward Seattle will leave at four-thirty. We won't get there in time if Ralston plans to leave on the four-thirty ferry, but Ryker will."

"I'll call him," Parker offered.

Waiting to hear back from Ryker after Parker called him and explained the situation was nerve-racking, to say the least. In a perfect world, theoretically, if the four-thirty ferry didn't board until after the ferry from Seattle that Ryker was arriving on unloaded, Ryker should have time to find Riley and Ralston in line before they slipped away. Not that he'd ever met Ralston or Riley or even knew what they looked like, but Phoenix had forwarded photos of both of them to him.

"It's Ryker," Parker said when her cell phone rang at four-forty. She answered. "Did you find them?"

We all waited while she listened.

"No kidding," she said. "Okay. I'll see you when you get here, and thanks."

She hung up and looked at the rest of us, who waited to hear what she had to say. "Ryker said Riley and Ralston were at the ferry terminal to pick Ilia up. Apparently, Ilia had been in Seattle for court-mandated visitation with her father and was on her way home. Her mother was supposed to meet her at the ferry terminal and give her a ride home, but her mother was sick, so Ilia called Riley and asked if she could borrow a car from her mother or her sister and come and pick her up. Since Riley was with Ralston when she received the call, he offered to take her to pick her friend up."

I was pretty sure my mouth was hanging open in disbelief by this point. While the story could be true, it also seemed unlikely.

"Ilia is required to go to Seattle twice a month for court-mandated visitation with her father, who is a real tool if you ask me, so the fact that she was in Seattle visiting him is entirely believable," Phoenix verified. "And it's also true that Ilia's mother has been battling cancer and has good days and bad, so Ilia needing a ride isn't all that unusual. But if all that is true, why was Riley's phone set on the 'do not disturb' mode?"

"She told Ryker she didn't know it was set on 'do not disturb,'" Parker answered. "She said she must have forgotten to turn it back on after school."

"It sounds as if that part of Riley's story might be a lie, but I guess you'll need to ask her about that," I suggested.

"So where is Riley now?" Phoenix asked.

"She left with Ilia and Ralston. Ryker didn't have any reason to detain her. He did say that he suggested that she call you to check in, but he had no way of knowing if she would. There's something more," Parker said.

"Something more?" I asked.

"Ryker shared that Ralston gave him a look when he stopped him to inquire about the reason for his presence at the ferry terminal with Riley. While everything Ralston said seemed above board, Ryker also said the guy had this look about him. It was a look Ryker's seen before on other psychopaths. He doesn't think Riley is in any immediate danger, but he does think we're right to be concerned. He suggested that we sit down and discuss everything we know with him and offered to brainstorm with us to devise a strategy. At this point, Ryker is of the mind that the guy is playing with us. He's enjoying the game, and the game alone is likely enough for him for the time being, but at some point, he'll grow bored."

"And what happens then?" Phoenix asked. "When he grows bored?"

"Nothing good," Parker predicted.

Chapter 11

By the time Ryker showed up, Coop had arrived with Hank. Phoenix had gone home to care for her younger siblings since the babysitter had to leave, and Riley hadn't shown up yet.

Adam called me shortly after Ryker called Parker with his update from the ferry terminal to let me know that he and Hudson planned to visit Justice before spending the rest of the evening with the boys at the academy. He was sorry to have to cancel our tentative date, but he promised to call me later so we could catch up. While I was disappointed that he wouldn't be joining us this evening, I fully understood his need to be available for the boys. It was a beautiful day, and I decided to enjoy the friends I was with, so I grabbed a few bottles of the wine my uncle, Warren Cornwall, had sent, and then Jemma,

Coop, Parker, Ryker, Josie, and the animals joined me on the deck of the roommates' cottage.

"I keep thinking that we're missing something obvious," I said to the group as I passed out glasses of the first of several wines I planned to offer. "Ralston seems to be the calculating sort. If I had to guess, everything he does and says has been planned out in advance. He knows he has us hooked, and I suspect he's confident in his ability to outsmart us and in no way sees us as a threat. He's playing with us. Reeling us in and then letting us out just enough to keep things interesting."

"I'd say that's an accurate depiction of the guy," Parker agreed. "So, how do we get the upper hand?"

Once I'd poured myself a glass of wine, I sat down with the others. "The information Ralston has dropped about his past seems inconsistent, but as I said, Ralston seems to be a calculating sort of guy, so it seems to me that the inconsistency might be on our ability to process the clues he's provided and not his delivery of the clues."

"You think that some of the information he's provided to this point that we've classified as being irrelevant and have since discounted might actually be important," Parker confirmed.

I nodded. "An example of this would be that the guy specifically mentioned Panguitch, Utah, as his residence before he migrated to Gooseberry Bay. Our efforts to find any reference to the guy living in Utah under any of the aliases we know of were unsuccessful, but what if he mentioned that specific town for another reason. What if he told Phoenix's mom that he'd moved to Gooseberry Bay from Panguitch, Utah because he wanted us to look there for clues."

"That makes sense," Ryker said. "If Ralston is all about the game and less about the kill, he'll want those of you he's managed to snag to have enough clues to make the game challenging."

"So maybe we should take another look," Jemma suggested. "I have my laptop inside. I'll grab it and set it up on the table out here."

Jemma grabbed her laptop, logged in, opened her preferred browser, and then asked the group where she should begin her search.

"We know that Ralston first showed up here in March, so let's search for significant events between October of last year and March of this year that may have taken place in or near Panguitch, Utah," Parker suggested.

"Significant events?" Jemma asked.

Parker replied. "Murders, kidnappings, missing people, thefts, little old women who had been stripped of their life savings, that sort of thing. We really don't know why Ralston is here or what it is that he's after, but I have this feeling that his reason for being here is going to be to do something that is going to be significant enough to make the local news."

Jemma began searching, and after a few minutes, she sat back and merely stared at the screen.

"What is it?" I asked.

"Jillian Riverton of Panguitch, Utah was found dead on November nineteenth of two thousand twenty-four," Jemma read. "She was a high school senior and was last seen leaving volleyball practice, where she was a starter for the high school team. Her body was found behind the equipment shed by one of the football coaches the day after she was reported missing by her sister, Veronica."

"This is bad," Josie said. "Did they ever find the killer?"

Jemma shook her head. She then paused and shrugged. "The answer to that is inconclusive. It seems that Jillian lived in a dysfunctional sort of situation. Her mother was an alcoholic, who, according to the report filed by the investigating officer, was passed out on the sofa after a day of drinking on the day Jillian failed to show up from school. Jillian's father had taken off a few years earlier, and while the couple was still legally married, the husband lived in the next town over, and he really wasn't in the picture. Veronica called the police when Jillian failed to come home after practice. The police officer who responded to the call took down some information but wasn't overly concerned. Jillian was seventeen and a high school senior. Kids that age took off sometimes, according to the cop, at least."

"I take it the report you found was filed by someone other than the officer who first responded to Veronica's call," Coop said.

Jemma nodded. "Once the body was found, a detective was assigned the case. He's the one who wrote the report I'm referring to."

"How did you get access to that report?" Ryker asked.

Jemma smiled. "I have my ways."

I supposed Ryker could make trouble for Jemma if he took exception to her digging around in police files she shouldn't have had access to, but he seemed like a cool guy who would hopefully turn a blind eye.

"Is there any reference to Ralston?" I asked.

"Not that I can see from this report. The father, who worked in a town just fifteen miles away, was a suspect for a minute after a friend of Jillian's told the police that he'd been in town for some reason and Jillian had confronted him in a local bar. She warned him to get out of town and leave her mother alone, but he didn't take well to being sassed by his daughter. He slapped her, and she left."

"Did the father have an alibi for the time of the murder?" I asked.

"He did. Or at least he had a friend willing to provide an alibi. Based on the report filed by the detective who investigated the death by strangulation, he never was convinced that the father hadn't done it."

"Were there other suspects?" Josie asked.

Jemma looked at her screen, scanning down a bit as she searched for the information she hoped to find. "Jillian's boss was questioned, as was a neighbor who had only recently moved into the neighborhood."

"And why were they questioned?" I asked.

"Jillian's boss, the man who owned the burger joint where she worked on weekends, was known in the community for being a bit of a perv who others reported came onto his young staff at times, and the neighbor, a man named Samuel Hightower, had befriended Jillian and Veronica told police that the guy seemed a bit too polished for her taste."

"Samuel Hightower!" Parker screeched.

"Does that name mean something?" Ryker asked.

"The driver's license in Ralston's wallet has his photo, but instead of his name, it has Keith Hilton on it. We found this odd, so we looked into it. Keith Hilton lives in Santa Fe, New Mexico. He's sixty-two. Keith has a son named Samuel. Apparently, Samuel, who is thirty-two, took his mother's surname when his parents divorced. His mother's name was Joanna Richardson. Joanna's father was named Ralston Richardson. Samuel's middle name is Ralston. We figured that the Ralston Richardson currently living in Gooseberry Bay is actually Samuel Ralston Hilton, who changed his name to Samuel Ralston Richardson after his parents' divorce. But here's the real kicker, I did some more digging into Keith Hilton, who, by the way, is dead, and found out that Keith Hilton's middle name was Hightower, after his mother, whose maiden name was Hightower."

"It seems as if Ralston has a bunch of aliases, but he seems to hang onto parts of his name or at least parts of his family name with each incarnation," I added. "He told Phoenix's mother that his name was Ralston Richardson, he leased an apartment under the name Keith Hilton, which matches the driver's license he's carrying around, and now it sounds as if he might have rented a house in Panguitch, Utah under the name Samuel Hightower. Additionally, he has four credit cards in his wallet, all assigned to men recently deceased and all with different names."

"If we can't get him for murder, I can probably pick him up for credit card fraud, but I'm not sure that's our best move," Ryker said. "If the guy did kill this young woman, he's likely killed others. The downside of bringing him in on the fraud charge is that he'll likely stop feeding you clues. He seems to be enjoying the game he's playing with you. My gut instinct is to allow him to play a while longer."

"What if Riley is his next victim?" Josie asked. "I don't think we can risk it."

Ryker responded. "I planned to take a backseat during this trip since this isn't officially an FBI case, and I haven't officially been asked to look into it, but with all we have, I think it might be time to call Lake." Special Agent in Charge Lake Bristow was Ryker's boss. "She'll probably agree that I have reasonable cause to dig around a little. If I get her okay, I can access files only available to law enforcement." He glanced at Jemma. "Or perhaps only available to law enforcement or hackers of law enforcement agencies."

Jemma offered a weak smile but didn't say a thing.

Ryker went inside to make his call. After he came back out onto the deck, he filled us in. "Agent Bristow gave me the green light to dig around in an official capacity, and if I find enough to justify that we open a case, she's willing to do that. She suggested that, in the meantime, I round up all the members of Phoenix's family and then put a security detail on the house."

"I'll call Phoenix and ask her if Riley is home," I offered.

"And verify that her mom has come home from work as well," Parker added.

"And that Ralston isn't there," Josie pipped in.

A call to Phoenix provided the information that Phoenix, Riley, and their mother were all at home and that Ralston had departed after dropping Riley off. Riley told Phoenix that Ralston was tied up that evening, and they wouldn't see him until the following day. Ryker still wanted the house watched, so he called Deputy Dani Dixon as one law enforcement individual to another, and she agreed to have someone drive by the house a few times before the end of the current shift but shared that she was already shorthanded due to having Justice, who needed twenty-four-hour monitoring, in custody.

I called Phoenix and updated her on the situation. She managed to get her mom to take the younger kids to her sister's house, and I suggested that Phoenix and Riley come and stay with me. Phoenix agreed to my plan but couldn't convince Riley to come and stay on the peninsula. She was, however, able to persuade her to stay at Adam's estate. Since Riley hung out there a lot, and Phoenix had stayed there quite often in the past as well, she called Adam, who was okay with the arrangement.

Chapter 12

Last night had been both eye-opening and disturbing. Once Ryker got involved and logged into his computer, he found four additional instances where a high school student was strangled and then left for dead, either at the high school she attended or near the high school she attended. In addition to Jillian Riverton, who died six months ago, we'd been able to identify Tasha Braveheart of Nogales, Arizona, who died a year ago, Elizabeth Livingston of Cortez, Colorado, who died eighteen months ago, Lydia James of Longview, Washington, who died two years ago, and Rosemary Gibbs of Santa Fe, New Mexico, who died three years ago. While the fact that Justice's sister fit the profile terrified me, it also encouraged me. If Justice's sister was killed by Ralston, then Oberson hadn't actually done it as Justice suspected. Initially, I hoped that would let

Justice off the hook, but then I realized Justice believed Oberson had done it whether he had or not, so his belief still provided him with a motive to kill the new substitute teacher.

Ryker felt there were likely other victims besides the ones he'd dug up, but the names he came up with were enough to establish a reasonable cause to open an official investigation. Ryker went by the apartment Ralston Richardson had leased as Keith Hilton, but no one was there. In fact, from the outside, it appeared that the place had been cleaned out, which probably meant that Ralston had decided the game had become much too risky with Ryker's presence and had fled before anyone could catch up with him. At least he hadn't had the chance to kill anyone in Gooseberry Bay before taking off. Or had he?

"What if Ralston killed Oberson?" I asked the group the following morning. Since Coop had a charter today, he'd left Hank with Jemma and then headed toward the airfield, so it was just Jemma, Josie, Parker, Ryker, the animals, and me for breakfast that morning.

"Oberson isn't a teenage girl," Parker pointed out.

"No, he's not, but other than the fact that he isn't a teenage girl, the profile still fits. He was strangled to death, as were the other likely victims of Ralston, who we've identified, and he was left on the high school property. He was even left beneath the bleachers, which happens to be the same location where Justice's sister was found at the high school she attended."

"Interesting theory," Ryker said as he sliced into a stack of pancakes. "While Oberson most definitely doesn't fit the profile, it is true that he taught at the school Lydia James attended when she died. Maybe he saw something or knew something about Lydia's death. Something he either kept to himself for some reason or perhaps something he used to blackmail Ralston at the time of the murder if, in fact, it had been Ralston and not Oberson or the boyfriend who killed Lydia."

"So Ralston is here in Gooseberry Bay to stalk out his next victim, and, quite by chance, he runs into Oberson after the man comes to the area to fill in for a teacher who's out on maternity leave. Ralston either has a grudge against him in need of settling or feels threatened by the man, so he kills him," Jemma said.

"Seems like a theory that works to me," Ryker said. "Of course, a theory that works isn't proof and won't get Justice off the hook."

I took a moment to think things over. Something about this whole thing didn't seem to fit. In the past, I've often found it helpful to verbalize my thoughts and let others chime in when I needed help organizing them.

"It seems to me that Ralston Richardson, or whatever his name is, has a type," I started. "Lydia James was a high school student from a dysfunctional home. Her mother died, and her father was an alcoholic. Not only did she need to raise herself, but she was also responsible for raising her younger brother." I looked down at my notes. "Tasha Braveheart likewise was a high school student living

135

in a dysfunctional situation. Her father was abusive toward her mother, who refused to press charges, and Tasha was left not only defending her mother from her father but protecting the younger children in the household as well." I paused and took a breath, and then continued. "Elizabeth Livingston wasn't abused, but her mother worked three jobs and still wasn't able to make ends meet. Elizabeth was not only alone most of the time, but she and her mother were living in their car when she went missing. Rosemary Gibbs' mother was a prostitute who used to bring men to the house when Rosemary was home. According to the report, it seemed that some of those men preferred a younger partner and asked to have Rosemary subbed in on occasion. None of Ralston's possible victims, at least none who we've managed to identify to this point, lived in functional households. It's quite likely that Ralston sees himself as a savior of sorts. He rescues these girls from terrible lives by ending their torment."

"That's crazy," Josie said. "These girls were all juniors or seniors in high school. They were on the verge of being able to save themselves. Ralston didn't do them any favors by killing them to liberate them."

"I don't disagree, but if any of this is true, then I think we've established that Ralston is crazy," I stated.

"You know," Jemma said. "While most of this makes sense to me, the part about Oberson blackmailing Ralston doesn't. If Oberson knew that Ralston had killed Lydia and he used what he knew to blackmail the guy, I suspect that Ralston would have just killed Oberson right there on the spot."

There was a general consensus in the room that was likely true.

"Maybe Ralston simply recognized Oberson and figured that since he likely knew him, he could be a problem and killed him," Parker suggested.

"Or maybe," I countered, "Ralston was going to kill Lydia, but Oberson found out that she planned to spill the beans about his affair with her friend and beat Ralston to it."

"If that's the case, I'm betting he didn't like that," Josie said.

"It seems we have a lot of theories, but unless we come up with some proof to back those theories, we really don't have anything," Ryker said. "I plan to get a warrant to search Ralston's apartment. I'll talk to his neighbors and try to come up with something concrete."

"I'll go with you," Parker said.

Jemma, Josie, and I decided to do some more digging while Parker and Ryker were away. We had just settled at the dining table to go over our notes and come up with a strategy moving forward when Deborah Goldfield called to let me know that her friend, Glorene, had offered to not only pick her up from the hospital but to stay with her for a few days, allowing her to go home earlier than first predicted. She was at home now and wondered if I could bring her husband by. I agreed to do so and left Jemma and

Josie brainstorming solutions to the Ralston Richardson problem while I made the quick trip into town.

When I arrived at Deborah's home, I knocked on the door, and Glorene answered. She invited me in, so I decided to stay for a few minutes. Deborah was pretty beaten up, but the smile on her face when I greeted her seemed to indicate that she was in good spirits.

"Thank you so much for going to so much trouble to return Harold to me." She hugged the urn to her chest. "I don't know what I would have done if you hadn't found me."

"I was happy to do my part, but it was actually Romy Mansfield, the woman from the bus, who saved the day by taking such good care of your tote bag and its contents."

"Yes, I owe a great debt to Romy. I spoke to her on the phone, but I'm not sure a mere 'thank you' is enough. Maybe flowers."

"Flowers would be nice."

"And you? I want to pay you something for your time."

I shook my head. "There is absolutely no need for that. I had time to poke around a bit, so when Romy asked me to help locate you, I agreed, but there was never a contract for services rendered, so no fee is due."

"Well, thank you. At least stay for a glass of fresh squeezed lemonade."

"That sounds nice."

After Glorine offered to fetch it, I settled on a chair adjacent to the sofa where Deborah was sitting.

"So, what are your plans for Harold now that you have him?"

She lovingly caressed the urn. "Harold wanted to have his ashes spread over the bay. He loved to fish, not that he ever really pulled anything out of the bay, but he liked to go out there and toss in a line as he whiled away a lazy afternoon. I can't do much in my current state, but once I'm feeling better, I imagine I'll rent a boat and do as he asked."

"My boyfriend has a boat, and when you're ready, he and I would be happy to take you and whomever else you'd like to bring out into the bay with you. He has a large boat. Really more of a yacht, so inviting friends and family along shouldn't be a problem."

The woman wiped a tear from her cheek. "Why thank you, dear. That is a very generous offer, and I might take you up on it. While I don't have much family, Harold did have a few friends I'd like to invite to come along."

It was sad, and I felt so bad that she didn't have much of a family. She was of an age when parents had likely passed, and siblings might have as well, but the way she said what she had led me to believe that children, nieces, and nephews weren't in the picture.

I handed her one of my cards. "All my numbers are on here, including my personal cell phone. Call me any time, and we can make the arrangements."

I drank my lemonade and chatted with Deborah and Glorene for about half an hour before I said my goodbyes and left. After I left Deborah's house, I realized I'd forgotten to do something when I'd stopped at my office to pick up the urn with Harold's ashes. I'd left a few files in a desk drawer that I'd feel better about locking up in the file cabinet, and since transferring them from one location to another would only take a few minutes, I decided to head back to my office. When I arrived, I found that someone had slid a manilla envelope under the door that opened into the hallway I shared with the animal adoption center, Hair Affair, and Gooseberry Yogurt. Whenever one of the businesses that shared the space was open, the general public had access to the hallway leading to a public restroom. The pet adoption center, beauty salon, and yogurt shop were open today, so I supposed I could ask the staff at those three locations if they'd noticed anyone at my door in the last hour or so. I didn't want to make a big deal out of it if the envelope held a flyer or ad of some sort, so I transferred my files so I wouldn't forget to do so, and then I opened the envelope. There was a single sheet of paper with four words written on it.

Riley isn't the target.

Chapter 13

"I know we've been assuming that Riley is the target since Ralston has been paying so much attention to her, but she doesn't fit the profile," I said, directing my comment to Jemma and Josie after I returned to their cottage. "The other girls all lived in volatile living situations. While it is true that Riley's parents were recently divorced, it was an amicable divorce. The kids see both parents. The kids are all loved and cared for. No one drinks or does drugs, and as far as I know, there has never been any violence in the household. If Ralston's goal is to liberate teens from dysfunctional homes, he wouldn't have chosen Riley."

"Then who?" Josie asked.

"I'm not sure," I admitted. "I'm not even sure how we'd go about finding out. We could start with the high school and try to identify girls who fit the profile, but that would take forever, and even if we had the time and manpower, we'd have to be able to get inside Ralston's mind and gain some insight about what it is that causes him to choose one girl over another."

"He would have to have access to the girl of his choice," Jemma pointed out. "That is what made Riley such a good target. But if not Riley, then it has to be someone he had the opportunity to come into contact with. Maybe a teenage girl who lives in the same apartment complex as he does or someone who works at the burger joint where he likes to grab a quick meal."

"Or the friend of someone he knows well," Josie suggested.

"Ilia," I said.

"Ilia does fit the profile," Jemma agreed. "And Phoenix mentioned that she was at their house a lot since her home situation was so bad."

"Phoenix gave me her cell phone number, but she didn't answer, so I left a message. She never called back, but I'll try again," I offered.

Unfortunately, Ilia still didn't answer. That didn't necessarily mean that the girl was in trouble. Ilia could just be involved in a task where she didn't want to be disturbed. I took a moment to fill Phoenix in on the situation, and she offered to go by Ilia's house to check on things. I knew Phoenix was at Adam's estate, and it would be at least a half hour until she could get there, so I told her to sit tight and that

Jemma, Josie, and I would head to Ilia's house and then call her with our findings.

"This is the address Phoenix gave me," I said to the others as we sat in Jemma's car in front of a run-down little house. "I'll knock on the door while both of you wait here."

I carefully made my way up the cracked sidewalk and knocked on the door.

"Who is it?" a voice called from inside.

"My name is Ainsley Holloway. I'm a friend of Riley's and would like to speak to Ilia," I called back.

"Not here."

I hesitated. "Okay. Do you know where Ilia is or when she'll be back?" I called once again through the still-closed door.

"Don't know. I need to rest, so if you'll kindly leave me to it."

"Uh, sure. I'm sorry to have disturbed you."

I had an odd feeling about things, but Phoenix had said that the woman was fighting cancer, so she may just have been too under the weather to get up and open the door. I supposed it might not be a bad idea to have Phoenix and Riley stop by after all. The woman might be more willing to let someone she knew well into her home rather than a total stranger.

"So what now?" I asked the others.

"Let's go back to the cottage and call Parker. If Ryker got the search warrant or they've spoken with the guy's neighbors, she and Ryker may have discovered something useful."

I thought back to our search of Clark Oberson's motel room. We hadn't found much, a poker chip, deck of cards, and bag of money, but I still wondered if it might have served our purpose to look into things further. We'd given Deputy Dixon the money we'd found. I was curious if she'd figured out why Oberson had it. Maybe following up at this point wasn't the worst idea. I'd have Parker do it since she and Dixon were friends while the deputy and I were still getting to know each other.

Parker called to let us know that Ryker had managed to get the search warrant he was after, but it had taken longer than they'd expected. They were heading to Ralston's apartment, and she promised to call me when they were done. I shared the note I'd found in my office with her, and she promised to share the information with Ryker.

Since it didn't seem like there was much for us to do until Parker and Ryker returned, Jemma, Josie, and I decided we would have time to take the dogs for a short walk along the beach that hugged the bay. It was such a nice day, too good to waste.

"I don't suppose you ever heard anything about the cash we found in Oberson's hotel room," I said, directing my comment to Jemma.

"I haven't heard a thing. Maybe Parker knows something. She seems to have established a relationship with our new deputy."

"Maybe. I intended to ask Parker if she's spoken to Deputy Dixon since we found the money, but there has been so much going on that I keep forgetting."

"I doubt that it will take long to search Ralston's apartment now that Ryker has a search warrant," Jemma said. "We'll ask Parker about the money when they get here."

Parker showed up with Ryker an hour later. They'd taken numerous photos, which Ryker downloaded onto his computer, and then he sent them to the TV screen. He wanted me to look at the downloaded images to see if I noticed anything that might stand out. I was willing to do so, but I didn't really know Ralston and wouldn't know whether or not something looked off. After a bit of discussion, we decided to go ahead and ask Phoenix and Riley to come over for an hour and help us sort through the photos in the hope of finding whatever the psychopath left behind for us to discover.

"By the way, I've been wondering if you ever heard back from Deputy Dixon about the money we found in Oberson's motel room," I decided to bring the subject up with Parker before I forgot to do it.

"She still isn't sure where it came from, but she thinks it might be related to a high-stakes poker game that seems to float around the area. The game moves so often that law enforcement hasn't ever been able to keep up with it, but Dani seemed to think that the amount of cash you found most likely wasn't earned but was either stolen or won."

"Since he's the victim and not the killer, I suppose that knowing where the money came from isn't all that important," Jemma pointed out.

Josie decided to put some snacks out. It was remarkable that the woman maintained her slender figure since she constantly offered snacks. She was the high-energy sort and was usually busy with one thing or another, so perhaps she just burned off all the calories she consumed.

"Thanks for coming over," I said to Phoenix and Riley when they arrived. "I know it's a bit of a car ride."

"We're happy to help," Phoenix said.

"Phoenix is happy to help. I think this whole thing is dumb and a waste of time," Riley said before stomping across the room and flopping down on the sofa. Damon trotted over to say hi, which softened her mood a bit.

"So, how can we help?" Phoenix asked.

"We took a bunch of photos of the interior of Ralston Richardson's apartment, and we'd like you to look at them and tell us if you notice anything," Ryker said.

"Don't you need a search warrant for that?" Riley challenged.

"We have a search warrant," Parker informed her. She looked Riley in the eye. "Based on what we've discovered, we have reason to believe that your friend, Ilia, might be in real trouble. You can help, or you can pout, but if you don't help and she dies, you'll never forgive yourself."

That seemed to snap Riley out of her mood. She apologized and promised to do what she could to help find her friend.

"How well did Ralston and Ilia know each other?" I asked Riley.

She shrugged. "Pretty good, I guess. Ilia has a complicated situation at home, and there are times when she needs a break. When she needs some time to breathe, she comes to my house. Ralston has been around a lot lately, and Ilia has been around a lot lately, so they know each other pretty well."

"Ralston took you to pick Ilia up at the ferry," Ryker said. "He dropped you off afterward. Was Ilia still with him?"

Riley nodded. "She was. I live the closest to the ferry. Ilia lives up in the Oak Hills neighborhood. I realize she isn't answering our calls, but Ralston wouldn't hurt her. She probably just turned her cell phone off and forgot to turn it back on."

"Does she turn her cell phone off often?" Ryker asked Riley.

She frowned. "No. Not really." She paused. "Ilia needs to be available to receive calls from her dad. He's a real control freak. If she doesn't either pick up when he calls or at least call him back within a couple of minutes, he threatens to sue for full custody and make her move in with him in Seattle. She hates him. There is no way she would ever do that."

"How old is Ilia?" Ryker asked.

"Sixteen. Almost seventeen. Even though Ilia's just a sophomore, we have AP chemistry together. We were paired up for lab and got to talking about how truly screwed up life can be at times. I felt sorry for her and invited her over. That was back in September. We've hung out together ever since."

"Do you think Ilia is comfortable enough to go somewhere with Ralston alone if he suggested an outing together after they'd dropped you off?" Ryker asked.

Riley hesitated. "I don't know. I guess she might since she knows the guy, and she and I have gone out with him for burgers a few times. Ilia is pretty shy, though. I'm not sure she'd want to go out with him by herself. Do you think that's what Ralston did? Asked her to go out somewhere after he dropped me off?"

"We aren't sure," Parker jumped in. "We just know that Ralston and Ilia are missing and aren't answering their cell phones."

Riley looked at her sister, who was sitting across the room. "I know that Phoenix thinks something is off about Ralston and that he might be a danger to Mom and our entire family, but she's wrong. Ralston is just a nice guy who likes to do nice things for the people he cares about."

"Mr. Richardson has stolen credit cards in his possession," Ryker said.

"So? A lot of very nice people steal credit cards. Sam and Dean stole credit cards."

Ryker lifted a brow. "Sam and Dean?"

"The TV show *Supernatural*," Phoenix provided. "And that was different. They used stolen credit cards to pay their way, but Sam and Dean were on a mission to save the world."

"Maybe Ralston is some sort of secret agent," Riley said. "Maybe he's here undercover."

"He's not," Phoenix said.

"You don't know that," Riley shot back.

I could see the sister thing would quickly get out of hand, so I suggested that Agent Ryker start showing us the photos he'd uploaded to the TV screen.

"What are we looking for?" Phoenix asked once again.

"Really, just anything that catches your eye," Ryker responded.

"The apartment is pretty barren," Phoenix said.

"It appears that Ralston has packed up and moved on, but he didn't take everything," Ryker said. "If you asked me, I'd say he was in a hurry and emptied the closet and dresser into his bag but didn't bother with items on tables or the floor."

"What's that?" Phoenix got up and pointed to an object on the floor.

"I'm not sure," Ryker responded.

"Can you zoom in?" I asked.

Ryker did as asked. While the object increased in size, it also became blurrier. It was hard to make it out, but it looked like a piece of material or maybe a sock.

"It's a headband," Riley said. "The cheerleaders started wearing these cool headbands to keep the hair out of their eyes after Emily M. broke her arm when Amber failed to catch her during the dismount from the pyramid after her hair blew into her eyes."

"Are you sure this is the same headband the cheerleaders wear?" Ryker asked.

Riley nodded. "See that light blue line over the dark blue background. It's a monogram. Each cheerleader has their name on their headbands. They each have five of them all in different colors."

Ryker looked at Parker. "Did you pick it up when we were there?"

"No. I didn't even notice it. It's all balled up under that end table."

Ryker manipulated the photo a bit more. "It's too blurry to make out any letters. In fact, I wouldn't even have known the light blue lines in the design were letters if Riley hadn't told us."

"Is Ilia a cheerleader?" I asked.

"No," Riley answered. "There are eight. Amber A., Amber C., Brittany, Emily M., Emily R., Hayden, Madison, and Pippa. I suppose the headband could have belonged to any of them."

"I'll go back for it," Parker said to Ryker. "You keep showing the girls the rest of the photos. Text me if you see something else you want me to grab."

"I'll go with you," I said to Parker. "Even though we suspect Ralston is long gone, you shouldn't go there alone."

When we arrived, we found the headband right where the photo indicated it would be. The headband was the same deep blue as the carpet, so I could understand why Parker and Ryker hadn't noticed it the first time they were here. I picked the headband up and looked at it. "Emily," I said.

"Emily M. or Emily R.?" Parker asked.

I shrugged. "No idea. It just says 'Emily.'" I took my cell phone out and called Phoenix since I didn't have Riley's number stored in my phone.

"Ask Riley about the Emilys," I said to her. "Find out about their home lives."

"Okay, hang on."

I could hear Phoenix ask Riley the question in the background. There was a bit of discussion, and then Phoenix came onto the line.

"Riley said that Emily M. lives with her aunt, who is mad that she was asked to take over custody of her niece when her mom went to prison on a drug charge and is often mean to her. Riley said that Emily M. often has bruises on her arms from where her cousin, Richie, pinches her. She also said that there was talk that the reason Emily M. broke her arm when she fell from the pyramid onto the mats below was because it was already weakened due to a previous break that wasn't listed anywhere in her medical records. Emily R. lives on the bay with both parents, four siblings, and two dogs. Her father is a doctor, and her mother is in real estate."

"If Ralston is looking for a teenager to save, he'd most likely go after Emily M. rather than Emily R. Parker and I need to check on her. Ask Riley if she has her cell phone number or address."

Riley wasn't really friends with her, so she didn't have her cell phone, but she knew where she lived. She described the street and the house. Ryker wanted us to wait for him, so we told him we'd meet him in front of the house.

Parker and I arrived first but were only a few minutes ahead of Ryker. He slipped into the backseat of Parker's car once he arrived.

"Since we don't have a search warrant and aren't sure how our inquiry will be received, I should go up and ask for Emily," I said to Ryker. "Or maybe Parker. We can use the headband and say that we found it and want to return it. Neither of us knows Emily, but we're definitely less intimidating than you are."

"Fine by me. Just see if Emily's home. If she is, I'm going to want to talk to her. If she isn't, see if anyone knows where she might be. Also, try to get her cell phone number if she isn't home now."

Parker suggested that we go together, and I agreed. Parker rang the bell, and when a woman who looked to be in her forties answered, I asked for

Emily. When the woman said she wasn't home, I explained about the headband. I also embellished the likelihood that Emily would get into trouble for losing part of her uniform if I couldn't give it to her. The aunt didn't seem to care and claimed she had no idea where her niece had gone, but she willingly gave me her cell phone number. I called it, but Emily M. didn't answer. Unlike Ilia's cell phone, which appeared to be turned off, Emily M.'s rang before it went to voicemail, indicating that it was turned on, but she'd merely been unable to answer.

"What now?" I asked.

"We track the cell phone," Ryker said. "My entire team is off this weekend, but I'm sure someone must be at the office who can track it for me."

"If the cell phone is turned on, which it seems to be, Jemma can do it," I said. "Let's head back to the cottage."

Jemma tracked the cell phone to a beach about three miles north of the cottage. Parker rode with Ryker, and I waited with the others at the cottage this time. I wasn't the sort who enjoyed sitting on the sidelines, but Ryker was the FBI, and he had the gun, and this was, after all, a story Parker had been assigned. Well, sort of. Parker had been assigned the story relating to Clark Oberson's death. By this point, however, I was convinced that Ralston Richardson and whatever exactly he was doing here in Gooseberry Bay was connected to Oberson's death.

Chapter 14

Parker and Ryker found Emily M. at the beach with her friends. She admitted that she'd befriended Ralston Richardson after meeting him through Ilia, who had made Ralston brownies and then asked her for a ride to deliver them. The teen also admitted that she'd been to his apartment with Ilia a couple times and had visited Ralston on her own a few days ago. Additionally, she'd admitted that she'd run into him at the high school a few times and had stopped to chat with him the previous week when he'd attended one of the cheerleading practices. When asked if she was involved in a romantic relationship with the guy, the teen swore she wasn't but shared that she suspected that Ilia might have feelings for the guy, although she didn't have any proof to back that up.

Parker asked Emily M. about the headband, and the teen insisted that all her headbands, including the blue one, could be accounted for and hadn't been lost. She didn't have it with her, but she kept close track of them since the cheerleading coach would fine the girls if they lost or damaged any part of their uniform. Parker asked her to take a photo of the headband and send it to her when she got home, and Emily said she would.

"So, if Emily M. is telling the truth, and if she does indeed have her headband, then the headband in Ralston's apartment must belong to Emily R.," I said once Parker and Ryker returned to the cottage.

"How many high school girls did this guy befriend?" Josie asked.

"I guess that might be part of his process," Ryker said. "He gets to know a bunch of girls attending any one school and then takes his time deciding who is the person most deserving of his help."

"You mean he takes his time figuring out who to kill," Phoenix clarified.

Ryker nodded. "Yes, he takes his time figuring out who he will release from their pain."

"At this point, it seems as if Ilia is most likely his target," I said. "We should also check on Emily R. and confirm she's okay. While she doesn't appear to be a likely candidate and may have been at Ralston's apartment with one of the other girls, it would be remiss of us not to at least check on her."

"I'll call her," Riley offered. "I have her phone number."

Riley called Emily R. and was told by her sister that she had gone to cheerleading camp that weekend. Emily M. hadn't said a thing about cheerleading camp, so Riley called Amber A., who confirmed there was no camp that weekend and that Emily R. had likely lied to her parents to cover up her actual plans. Riley then called Brittany, who said the same thing.

"So Emily R. lied to her parents about her weekend plans," Phoenix said. "The question is: did she lie to hang out with friends, spend time with a boy, go to a concert, or did she lie to take off with Ralston and get herself killed?"

"Ralston wouldn't be interested in Emily R.," Riley said. "She's spoiled, stuck up, and a real witch. Ralston is a nice guy who enjoys spending time with other nice people. I know you all think he killed all those girls and that he's going to kill someone he met here in Gooseberry Bay, but you're wrong. He wouldn't do that."

"It does seem that Ilia is the better candidate," Phoenix said, ignoring Riley's comment declaring that Ralston was nice. "And as far as we know, she has been missing since yesterday afternoon. I don't suppose there was anything in the police reports we found that indicates how long the murdered girls were missing before they were strangled."

"I don't remember if it said or not," Parker answered. "I guess that might be a good thing to know."

It was nearly five o'clock, and I had the distinct impression we were running out of time. Even if

Ralston didn't kill his victims right away, he likely didn't keep them for long. The last time that either Ilia or Emily R. had been seen by anyone we'd spoken to was yesterday afternoon. My gut instinct told me that it was likely that if Ralston did have a girl who he planned to kill, it would likely be this weekend.

"The guy we know as Ralston Richardson left the bodies of all the victims we identified at the high school the victim attended," I said to the group. "To me, that seems to be an important clue. It's not like the guy can just strangle someone there in the middle of the day when there are people around. He must take the girl to the high school after dark."

"It sounds like someone should stake out the high school," Josie said. "If we don't find Ralston or the two missing girls before dark, that is."

"A stakeout isn't a bad idea," I said. "There is only one driveway leading up to the high school, so keeping an eye on it would be easy enough."

"There's that dirt access road behind the football field," Riley said. "Quite a few kids with SUVs or trucks use it to access the fields."

"Okay, so we'll need lookouts in both the front and the back," I said.

"We'll discuss this again if we don't find the girls we're looking for in a couple hours," Ryker commented. "It's just after five o'clock now, and the sun doesn't go down until almost nine."

The group agreed to continue to try to find both Ilia and Emily R. as long as we had daylight and then to regroup and stake out the high school if it came down to that. Since we didn't know what time Ralston planned to strangle his victim, or even if it would be today, I imagined we'd need to stay until sunrise if he didn't show up sooner than that. Of course, if he spotted us, he'd likely not come at all. I couldn't help but wonder what the guy would do if he knew we were watching. Would he simply change his kill location or wait for a better opportunity to present itself?

"I'm going to make us something to eat," Josie announced. "We seem to be at a standstill at the moment, and if we do end up on an all-night stakeout, we will need to have fuel to keep our strength up."

"I'm going to take Riley back to Adam's," Phoenix announced. "I'd like her safely tucked away until this is resolved."

Riley rolled her eyes at her sister. "You know you're being ridiculous. I'm in no danger. At least not from Ralston. He's a nice guy. I don't know why you can't see that."

I knew the more we forced Riley to argue her position, the more she would dig in heels, so I figured it was best to let it go.

"Before you go," I said. "Is there anything you know about Emily R. that might not be obvious by looking at her life from the outside?"

Riley frowned. "What do you mean?"

I responded. "I agree that on the surface, Emily R. isn't a candidate for a serial killer who kills to rescue teens from a bad living situation. She has an intact family, plenty of money, a nice home, and many friends. But could something be happening behind the scenes we haven't considered?"

Riley seemed to be taking a moment to think things over before she answered. "Emily R. may have mentioned that her father is super strict a time or two. Not only is Emily R. expected to get straight A's in every subject every semester, but her father makes her take college classes online in addition to her high school classes. I was surprised she even had time to do cheerleading and mentioned it to Brittany at one point. Brittany told me that the only reason Emily R. does cheerleading is because her father is convinced that cheerleading will look good on her college applications."

That didn't sound fun, and I wouldn't be surprised to find out that Emily R. cracked under the pressure at some point, but I wasn't sure that Ralston would see a strict upbringing as a reason for liberation. Unless...

"Do you know if there are consequences for not getting straight A's or accomplishing other educational goals?" I asked Riley.

She shrugged. "I don't know. I guess there might be, but Emily R. and I aren't close enough that we would have talked about it. If you really want to know what's going on behind the scenes, ask Brittany."

"Do you have her cell phone number?"

She nodded. "I'll forward her contact information to you."

While Ilia still seemed to make the better victim in my mind, I figured it wouldn't hurt to learn all we could about Emily R. while we tried to figure out our next move.

Phoenix thought it was likely that she'd stay at Adam's with Riley to keep an eye on her, but she assured me that she'd be available by phone any time I needed her or had a question for Riley. She was frustrated that Riley wasn't taking this whole thing more seriously and was afraid that if Ralston called and asked her to meet up with him, she'd do so. Hence, her logic in deciding to stay with Riley rather than return to the peninsula.

Josie had a salad and casserole ready by the time the clock announced the six o'clock hour, so we all gathered to enjoy the food while we continued brainstorming. Unless we discovered a new clue, we had nothing more than a couple pretty good theories to go on. With the absence of a new clue appearing out of thin air, it was beginning to look like we'd be spending the night in our vehicles waiting for Ralston, as we'd discussed.

"I'm going to take Kai and Kallie out," I said to Jemma once the dinner was consumed and the dishes were loaded into the dishwasher. "I can take Hank as well."

"Hank does need to go out, but I'll go with you," she responded.

"When is Coop supposed to be back?" I wondered.

"He should have been here by now, but he texted a while ago and said the charter ran late and he wouldn't be here until around eight o'clock. I'd ask him to come along on the stakeout, but I suspect he will want some quiet time after a full day of jumping through hoops to make difficult tourists happy."

"It does seem as if he ends up with some pretty demanding guests."

"It's getting worse with the good weather. During the winter, he primarily engages with local clients and activities, and more often than not, those local clients are pretty kickback." Jemma's cell phone dinged, indicating that she had a text. "Speak of the devil, it's Coop. I guess he was approached at the airport by a man wanting a lift to the airport in Seattle. Coop wasn't going to do it, but the guy offered him a ridiculous amount of money for an easy hop across the Sound, so he changed his mind. He plans to fuel the bird and head out, but he wanted to let me know he would likely be much later than he'd originally indicated."

"Is it safe for Coop to fly after being out all day?"

"He's used to long days every now and then. And it isn't like he was in the air the entire time. The group he had today wanted to head to a private island. Coop took them to the island, landed, and then just sat around waiting for them to be ready to head back."

"That sounds boring."

"I'm sure it is."

When Jemma, the dogs, and I returned to the cottage, the others had decided the stakeout was a go. Parker and Ryker would head over in Ryker's truck and park near the fields in the back. Ryker thought the dirt access road that ran behind the school would be a more likely used route for someone bent on murder than the driveway off the street that accessed the parking lot in the front of the building.

Jemma, Josie, and the three dogs rode with me in my SUV. It was a bit crowded, but since Kai and Kallie were large dogs, I had the largest cargo area available, so squeezing Hank in wasn't difficult. Jemma assured me the cats would be okay, even if we were out all night.

Ryker helped me stake out the best place to park before he continued around to the back of the building. While he wanted us to be able to clearly see the front entrance should Ralston decide to enter the school property from the road in the front of the building rather than the dirt access road at the back of the building, he didn't want us to be noticed from the street, the driveway, or the parking lot. The fact that it would be dark soon and my SUV was black did help.

"I brought snacks," Josie said from the backseat where she'd volunteered to sit with Hank.

"Didn't we just eat?" I asked.

She tossed a bag of cheesy chips onto the front seat. "We did. But we're here on a stakeout. Stakeouts are like road trips. They almost demand that you chow down on anything and everything you would never normally consider eating during your usual everyday life."

"You consistently eat junk food," Jemma reminded her roommate.

"I do, but the two of you don't so enjoy it."

Jemma opened the bag of chips and took a few out. She handed the bag to me, and I did the same.

"It's so weird to be sitting here waiting for some guy to show up to kill a young woman from the local high school," Josie said after opening one of the bags of chips she brought. "I'm terrified for both the missing girls and really stressed out about what is to come, but there is something oddly exciting about being in the middle of things."

"I get it," I said. "I've been on a few stakeouts in my day, and while they can be boring, there is a certain thrill that comes with waiting for something really explosive to happen."

"I can't help but wonder how Parker is doing with this," Jemma said. "As far as I know, this is the first stakeout she's been on since the two of you staked out Sawyer on the night he died."

Now, that was a truly horrific night.

"I did think about that. I think it's a good thing that Parker's with Ryker. He tends to keep her distracted."

Josie leaned over the back of the front seat and switched out her bag of chips for ours.

My cell phone dinged, letting me know I had a message. Although there was a very slim chance that anyone who might be lurking around in the area would notice the light from the cell phone in the darkness, thereby giving away our position, I wanted to be extra careful due to the importance of our mission, so I pulled one of the blankets we'd brought over my head and read the text.

I removed the blanket from my head and looked at my friends. "That was Phoenix. She said that Riley spoke to Brittany, who called her after she got my message, and according to Brittany, Emily R. is fine." I'd called Brittany earlier and left a message, but she hadn't returned my call. I guess I didn't blame her. The girl didn't know me, so why should she share her secrets with me. "According to Brittany, Emily was apparently invited to go camping with some kids from school, so she lied to her parents about her plans for the weekend since she knew they'd make her stay home and study for finals if she told them the truth."

"Was Brittany sure that was where Emily R. went off to?" Jemma asked.

"Brittany told Riley that Emily R. had told her what she was doing yesterday when she asked to borrow a sleeping bag. Brittany took the sleeping bag to school and gave it to her yesterday morning. She tried to call Emily R. to confirm she'd followed through with her plans, even though she was pretty sure the camp might be too far out of range to get service. Riley told Phoenix that she knew a couple kids who were likely on the trip with Emily R. She was going to try texting everyone in the hope that someone would wander into a spot with service and one of the texts would go through."

"It sounds as if we're back to Ilia as the most likely victim based on what we know," Jemma said.

"It does sound that way," I agreed. "She was last seen driving away with Ralston after dropping Riley off at her house yesterday afternoon."

"I hope she's okay," Josie said from behind me.

"Yeah. Me too," I agreed. "I keep thinking about those other girls, and I remember how cocky Ralston has been about the whole thing. He seems to know what he's doing. He's confident and likely certain of his mission. There is no doubt in my mind that, given the opportunity, he'll complete the mission he set out to complete when he showed up in town months ago."

"I still don't get the psychology that allows this man to believe that he's doing these girls a favor," Josie said.

"At this point, I suppose we're only guessing at what is going on in the guy's mind, but if he is doing what he's been doing to help these girls, he's never going to stop unless someone stops him," I said.

"There certainly isn't a shortage of teenage girls living in unimaginable situations out there in the world," Jemma agreed.

"With such a large pool of candidates to choose from, I wonder why he seems to take so much time with each one," Josie commented.

"Maybe he really cares about them," Jemma said. "Maybe he wants to get to know his victims so that he's certain they're worthy of being saved before he saves them."

This had to be one of the most disturbing cases I'd ever worked on. I was committed to seeing this through to the end, but I honestly hoped this ended tonight. I didn't want to spend another day focused on the disturbing images floating around in my mind, which I was sure would haunt my dreams for weeks to come.

Chapter 15

Forty minutes later, my cell phone rang. "It's Phoenix," I announced to the others and answered. "Hey, Phoenix, what's up?"

"Ilia called Riley a while ago. She asked her for a ride. Riley asked her where she was, and she said that she'd been with Stephie, but Stephie had to go to her grandmother's for the rest of the weekend, so she couldn't hang out any longer. Riley thought it odd that Ilia would call and ask her for a ride since she didn't own her own car, but it was Saturday night. Initially, Riley figured that Ilia might have thought she could borrow one. Riley was about to explain she was being held captive by her sister and her sister's friends when Ilia asked Riley not to tell her brother about needing a ride. Ilia doesn't have a brother. At least she doesn't have a brother any longer. He died when he was a young child. Riley realized that the mention of her brother was likely Ilia warning her that someone was listening in, so Riley informed Ilia that she had my car and would be happy to pick her up. She warned her that it could be a while since she was hanging with Mongo, and she'd need to make the trip back into town." Mongo was one of Adam's former students. "Of course, both Riley and Ilia know that Mongo has graduated and is no longer living at the academy, but Riley figured Ralston wouldn't know that. Ilia seemed to pick up on the fact that the mention of Mongo was code and that Riley understood that Ilia was in trouble of some sort, so Ilia just told her to get there as quickly as she could and then gave her an address."

"Wow. Okay. Hang on. I'm going to conference Parker in."

Once Parker came on the line, Phoenix went over that part again. It was quickly decided that Riley would go and meet Ilia, but not before we outfitted her with a tracking device. I had some in my office, so we agreed that Parker and Ryker would stay where they were in the event this was all a decoy to pull us away from the high school, but Jemma, Josie, the dogs, and I would meet Phoenix and Riley at the bridge, where it crossed the bay. We planned to put a tracker in Phoenix's car and another on Riley's person. Phoenix was going to hide in the trunk of her car, which had a safety latch so she could get out at any point, and the gang and I were going to follow from a safe distance using the trackers, which would feed into an app on my cell phone. If we had a visual on Ralston at any point and could, therefore, know with a degree of certainty that this whole thing wasn't just a ruse to get us away from the high school, Parker and Ryker would leave their post and join us.

"It sounds like we have a good plan with backups built in to keep Phoenix and Riley safe, but I'm still nervous," Josie said as we drove toward the meeting place. "Even if we can follow them, how do we know that Ralston won't shoot them once they arrive at their destination before we can get there to help them?"

"I guess we don't know that," I admitted, becoming even more nervous about the whole thing than I already was. "In a way, it makes the most sense for Ryker to be the person hiding in the car's trunk, but if he goes along with Riley, then it's just us watching the high school."

"We need to call Dani," Jemma said. "In the beginning, I know we had reason to keep her out of this, but a lot has changed. Those of us who are not armed and not trained in hand-to-hand combat shouldn't be the ones facing down Ralston and putting our lives on the line."

I agreed, so I called Parker back and expressed our concern. She informed me that she and Ryker had had a very similar discussion once I'd hung up. They'd called Deputy Dani Dixon and filled her in. They'd devised a new plan she had been just about to call and share with me. She informed me that they were on the way to the bridge to meet us, and Dani and her team would take over the surveillance at the high school. Suddenly, the knot in my stomach that had threatened to choke me just a minute ago began to relax.

The pullout on the Gooseberry Bay side of the bridge that spanned Gooseberry Bay was about twenty minutes from the high school. We realized we'd be late meeting Ilia, so Riley called her back, but she didn't answer. This only added to the tension, which, by this point, was so thick you could almost see it.

Once Parker and Ryker caught up with us, Ryker climbed into Phoenix's trunk, Phoenix climbed in my SUV with Jemma, the dogs, and me, and Josie joined Parker in Ryker's truck. We secured the tracking devices I brought and tested them in the app. When the tracker we put on the car and the tracker we'd hidden in Riley's bra showed up on the map provided in the app, Riley was instructed to head toward the address Ilia had given her. Those of us in the backup vehicles were ordered to hang back. Ryker didn't want Ralston to notice Riley had company until he could get inside and arrest him.

"I wish I looked more like Riley so I could have gone instead of her," Phoenix said as we did our best to keep an appropriate distance away from the car Riley drove.

"If we'd had more time to plan this, we could have sent a cop with a wig to take her place," I agreed. "Ryker is in constant contact with Deputy Dixon. Once he confirms what is actually happening, I'm sure he'll be able to advise her how to proceed."

When Riley arrived at the address Ilia had given her, she called to let her know that she was there and that Ilia should come outside. Ryker instructed Riley not to get out of the car or go inside the house under any circumstances. When Ilia didn't answer, we all began to get nervous. Not that we weren't nervous before, but somehow, the fact that Ilia wasn't here to greet us made things twice as bad.

"I can hear Ilia calling out to me," Riley said after a minute. "She's calling for me to help her."

"Stay put," I said to Riley, who had linked her cell phone to all five of us who'd hung back.

"Ryker is getting out of the trunk," Riley informed us. "He's approaching the house."

I literally held my breath.

"He's coming out," Riley said. "He has Ilia." There was a moment of silence before Riley informed us that Ryker was helping Ilia into the back seat of the car she had driven.

"And Ralston?" Phoenix asked.

"I don't know. I don't see the guy."

We could hear rustling on the other end of the phone line. After a minute, Riley came back on. "Ilia is safe, but Ralston is gone. He's had both Ilia and Emily R. tied up inside the house since yesterday. I suspect he decided it was time to make his move and had Ilia call and ask me to come and get her. Once that was done, he tied her up and left with Emily R."

I felt my heart sink into my stomach.

"Do you know where he took her?" Parker asked.

Riley answered. "Ilia thinks he took her to the high school, but she isn't sure. He said something about the basement. Ryker's driving Phoenix's car now, and we're heading in that direction. Ryker also called Deputy Dixon and filled her in so she's well aware of the situation. I guess she'll meet up with Agent Ryker once we arrive at the high school, and they'll figure it out from there."

"Deputy Dixon is already monitoring things at the high school. If the basement is Ralston's intended destination, I don't see any way for him to get past her," I said. "How long ago did they leave?"

Riley answered. "Ilia said he left with Emily R. right after she called me."

I figured that was almost an hour and a half ago, and by that point, we'd already been staking out the high school, so we'd had both entrances covered, but it was pitch dark outside. Maybe Ralston had somehow managed to find a way in despite our best efforts to keep an eye on things. Maybe Emily R. was already dead.

After we arrived at the high school, we found Ryker speaking with Deputy Dixon. Dixon had already checked the basement and found it empty. Her team was focused on scouring the grounds, searching for evidence that indicated that Ralston had been here with Emily R. within the past couple of hours.

"I wish I had thought to bring my computer," Jemma said.

Parker, Phoenix, Riley, Ilia, Jemma, Josie, and I were all standing next to the vehicles, trying to stay out of the way while still being close enough to hear what was being said.

"I have mine," Parker informed her.

"Grab it," Jemma instructed. "I might be able to find the blueprints for this place online. Maybe there is another way in we don't know about."

Parker jogged over to Ryker's truck, grabbed her laptop, and handed it to Jemma, who used the hotspot on her cell phone to log in. She set the computer on the hood of my SUV and began to search for the original blueprints filed when the school was built and the modified blueprints created during the renovation a few years ago.

"Originally, a mechanical room was located in the basement," Jemma informed us. "When the school was remodeled, they used part of the basement for a staff lounge, so they sectioned off the lounge area, which is finished, from the storage area, which is not. The mechanical room ended up on the other side of the lounge area, so it was further sectioned off." Jemma frowned as she scanned in just a bit. "There is a hallway that leads between the three separate areas." She looked at me. "Go ask Deputy Dixon if her men searched all three areas of the sub-ground level space."

Jemma trotted over, spoke to Dixon, and then came trotting back. "She said that she wasn't aware of a third space used specifically for storage. They checked the lounge and the mechanical room."

I could hear Dixon on the radio, telling her guys to check the storage area. Ryker wandered over and asked to look at the blueprints Jemma had found, and then he took off running toward the building.

"It looks like an air vent runs from the basement between the mechanical room and the storage area. The vent then runs throughout the building and seems to open onto the roof of the old gym," Jemma informed us.

The old gym was located near the ballfields at the rear of the property.

"I'm not sure if the vent is large enough to squeeze through, but I can see how Ralston might have been able to access the roof of the old gym without anyone seeing him once it was dark," Jemma added. "We were watching the entrances, not the rooftops."

"I'm going to take a look," Parker said.

"I'm going with you," I said. "The rest of you wait here."

Parker and I set off at a pretty brisk pace. We'd parked in the lot at the front of the building, so we had to run around the main building to the old gym that was no longer in use.

"How do we get onto the roof?" I asked.

Parker looked up. "Ryker is already up there."

"Do you see anything?" I called up.

He called back. "There's a lock on the grate covering the vent, which still seems intact. I don't think anyone got in this way. If Ralston was here, he must have taken Emily R. somewhere more accessible. I'm coming down."

Parker and I waited while Ryker climbed down from the roof.

"What now?" Parker asked.

Ryker frowned. "I'm not sure. I doubt Ralston is here now if he ever was."

"As long as we're all the way back here already, let's look around the bleacher area. Ralston seems to like the bleachers as a dump location."

Ryker agreed, and while we didn't find anything, I did have this odd feeling.

"Maybe we should bring the dogs back here," I said. "They'll be able to smell what we can't see in the dark."

Ryker lifted a shoulder. "I guess it's worth a try."

I took my cell phone out and called Jemma.

"Are you still at the vehicles?" I asked.

"I am."

"I need you to bring Kai and Kallie to the football field. You can leave them off leash. They'll stay with you."

"Okay. Give me a few minutes, and we'll be there."

"Where are Dixon and her team?" I asked Ryker.

"The last I saw them, they were looking around inside."

"I know it seems unlikely that the dogs will find anything or anyone, but I have this feeling. Maybe you should contact the deputy and put her on alert."

I had to hand it to Ryker. He did as I asked and didn't even argue about civilians leaving the police work to the professionals.

Once the dogs arrived, I told them to find Emily R. Of course, the dogs had never met Emily R., but I knew that they'd recognize the fact that I was asking them to find a person and would seek out the scent of any person not standing with our group. It took them nearly ten minutes, but eventually, I heard Kai bark. As I followed the sound of Kai's barking, I almost tripped over Emily R.'s body. I assumed she was dead, but not wanting to make that assumption without checking, I bent down to check for a pulse.

"She has a faint pulse," I said to Parker and Ryker.

Ryker notified Deputy Dixon and then called for an ambulance. I sat down next to the teen, who was still with us, but barely, and hoped the ambulance would arrive in time.

Chapter 16

The doctor was amazed that Emily R. had lived through her ordeal. As the others had been, Emily R. had been strangled, but unlike the others who succumbed to their trauma, Emily R. had passed out cold but had still been alive when Ralston likely noticed us in the area or heard us looking around and fled. Emily R. was still in the hospital, but her prognosis was encouraging.

Unfortunately, Ralston was long gone. I was happy we'd saved Emily R.'s life but frustrated that the guy who almost ended it had escaped and was likely to kill again.

"Will the fact that Emily R. was able to confirm that it had been Ralston who kidnapped, tied her up, and tried to kill her be enough to convince Deputy

Dixon to set Justice free?" I asked Adam when I chatted with him on the phone Sunday morning.

"I don't know. Probably not. Just because Emily R. can testify that Ralston Richardson kidnapped and tried to kill her doesn't prove that he killed the other girls, and it certainly doesn't prove that he killed Clark Oberson. We need to track him down and get him to confess."

That did seem to be the plan foremost in my mind. The problem was that no one seemed to have any viable ideas about where the guy might have gone once he left Emily R. in the forested area behind the bleachers.

"Maybe the guy is still using the same four stolen credit cards he had in his wallet when Riley found them," I suggested. "He must have needed to buy fuel, food, or lodging by now. I know it's a long shot, but it seems like a worthwhile endeavor to ask Ryker or Dani to run them."

Adam agreed that it wouldn't hurt to check it out. Ryker was still with Parker, so I decided to walk over to Parker's cottage and start there.

When I knocked on Parker's door, she answered. She was wearing pajama bottoms and a t-shirt. Ryker was wearing the same attire even though it was after ten a.m. I couldn't help but wonder if Ryker had actually slept on the sofa as Parker had indicated he would but decided it wasn't my business, so I didn't ask.

"Any word on the location of Ralston Richardson?" I asked the pair.

"Not yet," Ryker answered.

"Are you checking charges on the four stolen cards he had in his wallet?" I asked.

Ryker confirmed that the cards were being monitored and hadn't been used. He also confirmed that the cell phone Ralston had been using during his stay in Gooseberry Bay had been turned off, and there was no sign of his ever having returned to the apartment where he'd been living. Ryker had issued a BOLO for his vehicle and included Ralston's description and a photo, but he wasn't expecting much. The guy had merely disappeared. He never seemed to hang onto any one identity for long, and he'd likely already stolen new credit cards to replace the ones he'd likely abandoned, so it was possible that tracking him down wouldn't happen until he surfaced again.

"Unless we catch a break," I said, ardently hoping that a break would be forthcoming.

"Or unless we catch a break," Parker parroted. "Do you want a cup of coffee?"

I could sense that, regardless of their relationship status, I'd interrupted an intimate morning between Parker and Ryker, so I declined the offer. I got up to head to the door when my cell phone rang. It was Phoenix.

"Hey, Phoenix. How is everyone this morning?"

"Mom is still in denial and is insisting that there must be more going on with Ralston than we realize since a nice man like that could never be a killer. But

Riley seems to have finally accepted that the guy she has been mooning over for the past few months is not the nice guy she thought he was."

"I'm glad that Riley at least is in touch with reality. It will make it easier to bring your mom around once she's ready to listen."

"I hope so. Anyway, I'm calling because Riley and I visited with Emily R. in the hospital this morning, and she asked about her cell phone. I told her that she didn't have a cell phone when we found her, and she said that she had it in the truck after Ralston left Ilia behind and took her to the high school. The teen remembered thinking she'd try to slip her cell phone out of her pocket and call someone if Ralston looked away or was distracted even for a moment. When Ralston looked down at his cell phone for a moment, she saw her chance, but just as she was pulling the cell phone out of her back pocket, Ralston turned and looked right at her. She panicked and stuffed it down in the seat between the back cushion and seat cushion. She's pretty sure it's still there."

"So maybe we can track it," Ryker said after I shared what Phoenix had told me. "Do you have the number?"

I asked Phoenix, and she rattled it off. Ryker called someone from his FBI team and asked to have the cell phone tracked. Surprisingly, he found that the cell phone was still in Gooseberry Bay. That didn't mean that Ralston or the truck he was driving were still in town since he might have dumped his truck or possibly found the cell phone and dumped it. Ryker announced that he needed to get dressed so that he could go and check it out, and Parker asked to go with him. I saw this as my cue to leave and did so.

Thirty minutes later, Parker called to let me know the truck had been found abandoned with the cell phone still inside. Fortunately, Ryker was able to track down a man who lived on the same street where Ralston's truck had been found, and the man reported that his car had been stolen from his driveway earlier that morning. The stolen car had a security system that allowed them to track the vehicle, which he'd done, only to discover that his car was currently on the ferry that crossed the sound between Gooseberry Bay and Seattle. Ryker called his partner, Agent Blade Branson, who was currently in Seattle, and asked him to meet the ferry on the Seattle side. Everyone hoped that Ralston would be arrested and interrogated, and we'd have the rest of the story and be able to close this case shortly after the ferry docked.

Chapter 17

A somber group met at the roommates' cottage for a brainstorming session a few hours later. While Agent Branson had been successful in apprehending Ralston Richardson and even getting him to confess to killing ten young women over the past five years, he wouldn't admit to having killed Clark Oberson. Ralston was, in fact, quite adamant that he only killed when the best interest of the victim demanded it, and he would never have wasted his time on a lowlife like Oberson. I believed him. Adam and Deputy Dixon both believed him. Unfortunately, however, without Ralston Richardson as a suspect, we were back to Justice as the most likely person to have murdered the new substitute teacher.

Adam and Hudson decided to come over and brainstorm with us while Archie and Andi held the fort down with the boys. Things had become much more intense now that our alternative suspect had turned out not to be a suspect.

"Oberson was only in town for a few days before he was murdered," I said to the group. "That indicates that it is likely that the killer was either someone intent on killing Oberson for the cash that was found in his motel room or someone from his past."

"I've been thinking about the cash angle," Parker said. "If Oberson stole the money or obtained it in some other illegal manner and was killed because of it, it seems to me he would have been shot and not strangled."

"Parker's right," I said. "Besides, if the cash was the motive, it would seem that the killer would have found it. It wasn't easy to find, but it wouldn't have been difficult, especially if you knew what you were looking for and suspected it was there."

"So we're back to someone like Justice with a personal ax to grind," Jemma said.

"Or," Ryker countered, "we're back to Justice because he had a really good reason to want the man dead and that he followed through with his impulse to make things right."

"It wasn't Justice," Josie insisted.

I had to admit that while I wished I had Josie's resolve, my faith in Justice's innocence was waning. "I realize that Oberson didn't kill Lydia, and it was, in fact, Ralston Richardson who killed her, but Justice believed it was Oberson, and he had good reason to believe what he did. Just because Oberson didn't actually kill his sister doesn't mean that Justice didn't kill the man based on his belief in his guilt."

I glanced at Adam. Based on the look of total defeat on his face, I could see that he was coming around to my way of thinking on this situation.

"Okay," Josie said. "Say that's true. It still seems to me that before we lock the kid away, effectively ruining his life, we really ought to have proof of some sort. Proof beyond the idea that since he had a good reason to do it, he likely did it."

"Josie is right," Hudson said. "I can feel a shift in the energy in this group, and based on everything that's happened, I understand that shift, but standing by while a good kid like Justice goes to prison without making sure we've explored every avenue of investigation doesn't seem right."

"I don't disagree with you," Jemma said. "But how do we find proof one way or the other?"

"Has anyone seen the official autopsy report?" Ryker asked. "If Oberson was strangled, you can learn a lot about the killer by studying the autopsy report, especially if the killer used his hands to do the strangling."

Everyone in the room agreed that the last any of us had heard, Dani was still waiting on the official autopsy report. While I understood that it was the weekend and that we lived in a small community with limited resources, it seemed to me that with a kid in jail waiting for someone to prove his innocence so he could go home, obtaining the information needed to make informed decisions really ought to be fast-tracked. Adam got up to call Dani, hoping to receive new information while the rest of us continued to chat.

"I realize that I've missed many discussions that everyone else has participated in over the past few days due to my charter schedule. But if I understand it correctly, the theory is that Oberson killed Justice's sister, Lydia, because she found out that Oberson, an adult and a teacher, had been sleeping with her best friend and threatened to tell someone in a position of authority," Coop said.

"That seems to be the case," I agreed. "The theory is that Justice thought it was Oberson who killed his sister to protect his job and reputation, and when Oberson wasn't arrested for her murder, Justice went crazy and took care of it himself."

"Do we know if the rumor about the affair between Oberson and Lydia's friend was true?" Coop asked.

I admitted I wasn't sure about that, but I had no reason to believe it wasn't true. "Why do you ask?"

Coop shrugged. "I guess I just wondered if Clark Oberson seduced other teenage girls."

"You think that he might have been killed because of a previous affair with a minor," Jemma stated.

"I guess I think it's a likely possibility," Coop confirmed. "I know the guy had only been in Gooseberry Bay for a few days before he was found dead, which is hardly enough time to become friends with and seduce a local teen, but I wonder if he acted in a substitute capacity for our local high school before."

Coop had brought up an idea that definitely deserved to be explored a bit further. If Oberson had spent time in Gooseberry Bay in the past, and if he seduced another teen during his time in our small town, might it be possible that it was the teen, or a friend or family member of the teen, who might have sought revenge?

"It's Sunday, so it will be hard to get Oberson's employment records, but I bet Dani can find out if the guy has worked in our district before," Parker said.

Parker stepped outside to call Dani just as Adam returned from speaking to her about the official autopsy report.

"According to Dani, the official autopsy report indicates that Clark Oberson was strangled with a strip of leather," Adam said.

"Leather?" I asked.

"A wide strip such as a cord or belt."

We were all disappointed that the autopsy report didn't come up with something a bit more helpful.

"Has anyone asked Justice if he knows anyone he might consider a suspect?" I asked. "Maybe he knows something that we don't, and perhaps he hasn't volunteered that information because he doesn't realize it's important, and no one has asked him about it."

"I'll go and talk to him," Adam offered.

"I should go," Ryker said. "I'm trained in conducting these sorts of interviews."

"I'll go with you," Parker said.

"I'm not sure he'll talk to you," Adam warned.

"Okay, then the three of us will go," Parker decided.

After Adam, Ryker, and Parker left to speak to Justice, Jemma, Josie, Coop, Hudson, and I decided to walk all the dogs. It felt as if it had been more than a month since Oberson was found dead, but in reality, it had only been three days.

"The fact that Oberson was found strangled and left beneath the bleachers at the high school rather than being shot or stabbed and dumped in the bay makes it appear that Justice is the one to have killed him," Coop pointed out. "Maybe we should be looking for individuals who not only had reason to want Oberson dead but for individuals who might want to frame Justice as well."

We had discussed that before, but I was somewhat sure that Coop hadn't been here when the subject had come up. Still, we had never followed through with the idea.

"The problem is that we really don't know Justice well enough to know who would want to frame him," I said.

"I know him pretty well," Hudson said.

"Okay. Then who might have the motive to frame Justice?" I asked.

Hudson stopped walking to think about it. We all paused to wait for him.

Eventually, Hudson spoke. "I recently learned that another kid who had been in juvey with Justice is in town. He is also from Tacoma. His name is Kurt Johnson. I'm not sure how long the kid has been in town or whether he has family here or is here for another reason, but I was with a few of the boys at the arcade maybe a week ago, and this kid comes up and pulls Justice aside. I didn't interfere, but I did keep an eye on them. The kid, who eventually lured Justice into the parking lot, seemed fairly upset about something. I was still trying to figure out whether or not I should step outside and get in the middle of things when Kurt left. I asked Justice who he was, and he told me his name. When I asked Justice how he knew the kid, he said they were friends when they were little and had both attended the same school in Tacoma, and then they both ended up in juvey at the same time. I asked him what Kurt was so upset about, and Justice said that Kurt wanted the spot at the academy that Justice ended up getting, and Kurt was sure that Justice stabbed him in the back to steal the opportunity that should have been his."

"Did he steal the spot from this kid?" I asked.

"No. Kurt's uncle applied to the academy on his behalf, but Kurt was never really considered due to his behavior problems, which included acts of violence against others. Additionally, his poor grades indicated a total lack of interest in anything academic.

When Justice's parole officer made the same application on Justice's behalf, Adam and Archie saw something different in his records and decided to give him the benefit of the doubt."

"I guess I can see why Kurt is bent out of shape," Jemma said.

"Yeah," Hudson agreed. "I suspect that having his application denied and Justice being accepted just a couple of months later was a hard pill to swallow."

We all started walking again.

"Okay, so Kurt seems to have a grudge to settle with Justice, but did he have a reason to kill Oberson?" Josie asked.

I suspected that was the question of the hour. "Johnson," I said aloud. "Lydia's friend who was having an affair with Oberson was named Collette Johnson. I know Johnson is a common name, but it seems it might be worth our time to figure out if Collette Johnson is Kurt Johnson's sister."

"So if Kurt and Justice were childhood friends who both ended up on the wrong path and both ended up in juvey together and if Kurt felt that Justice had taken something from him that he wanted, Kurt, who has a history of acting out in violence might have decided to get even. And if the new substitute teacher in town had an affair with Kurt's sister while teaching at the high school in Tacoma, that gives Kurt a motive to kill him. The argument Justice had with Oberson is most likely what gave Kurt the idea to do things the way it appears he might have in the first place," I said.

Everyone agreed.

"I need to call Adam." I took my cell phone out of my pocket and made the call, ardently hoping it wasn't too late to rectify an injustice.

Chapter 18

A Week Later

The sun had yet to rise from beyond the bluff, but I was awake and feeling antsy, so I slid quietly out from beneath the blankets, pulled my running clothes on, and tip-toed out the door with the dogs for an early morning jog. I opened the little closet off the front entry to search for my heavy sweatshirt since the overnight temperature had dipped a good thirty degrees from yesterday's high, and then, after I pulled it over my head, I returned to the kitchen to leave a note for Adam, who was still sleeping like a baby under the mountain of quilts where I'd left him.

Usually, I might have chosen to stay all snuggled up with Adam, but it had been a long and emotional couple of weeks, and it seemed like I just needed some time to process everything before Adam and I met the gang for brunch in three hours. As I set off toward the boardwalk, I reflected upon the events that had transpired during the past few days.

Justice had been able to confirm that Kurt was Collette's brother and that Kurt had every reason to hate Oberson, the man he blamed for taking his sister's virginity and then ruining her life. Collette had gone all in with Oberson when the affair started, even going so far as to provide him an alibi when her best friend died and to swear under oath that she and Oberson were just friends and that they'd never done anything inappropriate with one another. Of course, once Oberson's long-term substitute teaching position ended, he left town, and Collette never heard from him again. According to what Kurt told Justice during their time in juvey, Collette went into a deep depression after Oberson left town, got into drugs, and ended up overdosing. Kurt had been looking for payback of some sort ever since.

Of course, Justice had no proof that it had been Kurt who had killed Oberson and then tried to frame him, but he'd given Ryker enough information to allow him to do additional digging. Ryker asked for a second autopsy as well as access to Oberson's clothing and personal possessions. It took a bit of time, but eventually, the FBI lab found one of Kurt's prints on Oberson's leather belt. Apparently, Kurt had removed the belt and then used it to choke the life out of Oberson. For reasons unbeknownst to anyone, rather than taking the belt with him after dumping the body, he put it back on his victim. Maybe he feared someone would notice and think it odd if it was missing. Kurt wasn't talking at this point, so it was all speculation.

Kurt was arrested for Clark Oberson's murder, and Justice was released into Adam's custody. Dani had recommended that Justice hang out at the academy until the situation in town settled down, and Justice agreed to comply with whatever terms he was given.

"Hold up a bit," I called to the dogs as we approached the highway. They knew to stop and wait for me before crossing, but I still liked to stay on top of my verbal cues. Once I arrived at the intersection where the dogs and I had the choice of turning right onto Main Street and the boardwalk, left to head toward the Rosewood Inn and several other small lodging properties or businesses, or heading straight up the hill to the high school, I decided to go straight. I had to admit that my stomach clenched up just a bit when the dogs and I reached the football field and the bleachers, but then I turned and looked toward the east as the sun appeared from beyond the bluff and knew I'd made the right choice on this particular morning.

"Check out that color," I said to the dogs.

They sat down next to me and actually appeared to be looking at the sky.

As the sun rose, the colors of the sky reflected on the bay. It was, in a word, breathtaking.

Even though the colors faded as the sun continued to rise, I still watched. I thought about Deborah, who'd called me two days ago to inform me that she was feeling better and ready to plan a memorial for her husband. She wasn't planning anything extravagant. Just her friend, Glorene, and a couple of her husband's friends on a boat as they said goodbye and honored his last request to have his ashes spread over the bay.

I'd talked to Adam about it, and since we had planned to use his boat, he suggested we visit Deborah together and discuss the upcoming memorial, which we'd done yesterday. Adam had been so sweet when he spoke to Deborah about her needs. He'd wanted to make sure everything was perfect for this very special yet challenging day and had asked her about her thoughts regarding every aspect of the ceremony. Not only was Adam providing the yacht for the excursion that would take place a week from yesterday, but he also planned to provide flowers and food.

Once the sun had risen in the sky, I decided to head back to the cottage. Adam would likely be up by now, and it would be nice to have a few minutes to have coffee together before I needed to jump in the shower to prepare for the day ahead. As I jogged back toward the cottage, I thought about the long, lazy summer, which, at this point, seemed to be perched just on the edge of the horizon. Just yesterday, Josie had been informed that she'd been chosen as the official food truck and concession provider for the Movies on the Beach event. It was a big job, and I knew she'd need help, but Hudson, who would be off for the summer, had volunteered to help, as had Jemma and I. In fact, time permitting, I was sure the whole gang would pitch in. The entire Geek Squad would be home from college for the summer, and Phoenix had already hinted that she had a plan to get the guys to pitch in as well. I was sure that selling snacks to moviegoers wouldn't be the boys' first choice for things to do, but Phoenix could be very persuasive.

"We're back," I called out once the dogs and I had entered the cottage after our run.

"I'm making the bed. I'll be right out," Adam called back from the bedroom.

When he emerged, he'd already showered and dressed for the day.

"Coffee?" he asked.

I indicated that I'd love some coffee, so he poured me a mug of the hot brew and handed it to me.

"How was your run?"

"Nice," I answered. "The sunrise was exceptional."

"We get some gorgeous sunrises from the mansion with it being built up on the bluff the way it is."

I'd witnessed several of those sunrises but didn't say as much.

"I suppose I should jump in the shower. We'll need to head to the roommates' cottage in less than an hour." I took a sip of the coffee. "I'm looking forward to brunch. When I first moved to Gooseberry Bay, the gang from the peninsula had brunch together almost every Sunday, but the tradition seems to have faded ever since Tegan and Booker moved away."

"I guess things have changed over the past couple of years. Avery, Bexley, and Parker are only part-time residents, so most of the time, it's just Coop, Jemma, Josie, and you out here on the peninsula."

I supposed that was true. "At least everyone will be there today."

"Is Avery back from Alaska?" Adam asked.

"She is, and she plans to be here. Other than having a short conversation on the phone, I haven't spoken to her yet, but she mentioned that she'd be bringing a friend to brunch, so I'm looking forward to that. Avery never talks about friends. Other than work friends, of course. I guess I assumed that she didn't have any."

"I'm looking forward to meeting the friend and catching up with Avery. Are Bexley and Parker going to be here as well?" Adam asked.

"They both said they planned to show. In fact, I'm pretty sure that Parker and Ryker arrived while we were out last night, and I think both Bex and Remi plan to come over on the first ferry this morning. In fact, they're likely here by now."

"It's been a while since I've had the chance to visit with Bexley and Remi. I heard that Hope is planning to attend and that she plans to bring Jackson, who I haven't seen for a good six months."

"I guess Jackson is in town for the summer." I held my warm coffee mug to my chest, allowing the warmth to radiate off the mug and steep inside. I smiled. "It does sound as if the entire gang will be together today for the first time in a really long time."

Just saying that made me feel all warm and cozy inside. I loved all my friends and enjoyed getting together with them, both individually or in small groups. There was just something, however, about the magic that occurred when the whole family came together to break bread and share the details of their lives.

USA Today best-selling author Kathi Daley lives in beautiful Lake Tahoe with her husband, Ken. When she isn't writing, she likes spending time hiking the miles of desolate trails surrounding her home. Find out more about her books at **www.kathidaley.com**

Made in the USA
Las Vegas, NV
24 April 2025

21326246R00115